Also by Ali Sparkes:

Frozen in Time

Destination Earth

Wishful Thinking

Out of This World

The Unleashed series:

A Life and Death Job

Mind over Matter

Trick or Truth

Speak Evil

The Burning Beach

The Shapeshifter series:

Finding the Fox

Running the Risk

Going to Ground

Dowsing the Dead

Stirring the Storm

DARK SUMMER

Ali Sparkes

OXFORD
UNIVERSITY PRESS

OXFORD
UNIVERSITY PRESS

Great Clarendon Street, Oxford OX2 6DP

Oxford University Press is a department of the University of Oxford.
It furthers the University's objective of excellence in research, scholarship,
and education by publishing worldwide. Oxford is a registered trade mark of
Oxford University Press in the UK and in certain other countries

Copyright © Ali Sparkes 2009

The moral rights of the author have been asserted

Database right Oxford University Press (maker)

First published 2009
First published in this edition 2014

British Library Cataloguing in Publication Data

Data available

ISBN: 978-0-19-273719-9

1 3 5 7 9 10 8 6 4 2

Printed in Great Britain

For Simon

Acknowledgements:

With grateful thanks to Mick Bush, and the team
at Wookey Hole Caves, for help and advice, and to
Dany Bradshaw for essential information on
cave diving and cave rescue.

Chapter 1

I've-no-han-ky-in-my-hand-so-I'm-a-bo-gey-won-
  derland . . .
    Wo! Bogey wonderland—wo—oh—
    Wo! No hanky in my hand . . . Oh no!
I split my pants when I start to dance in bogey
  wonderland . . .

It was only when Kayleigh and Chanelle stopped boogie-ing and put their hands on their hips that Eddie realized he'd been singing out loud. He stopped. He shuffled uneasily, and pushed his hands deep into his fleece pockets as they all stared at him. Auntie Kath pursed her lips and raised one eyebrow. Damon, though, paid no attention. He was listening to his iPod and ignoring all of them as they stood in the queue to the caves.

  'Sorry,' muttered Eddie, feeling his ears get hot. 'I didn't realize that was out loud.'

1

'Don't worry, girls—go on.' Auntie Kath turned her back on Eddie and smiled at her daughters. 'Some people just don't appreciate talent. And look . . . other people think you're wonderful!'

The twins smirked and then went on with their dance routine and yes, people *were* watching, and smiling indulgently. Kayleigh and Chanelle were nine-year-old disco dance champions, after all. Three times a week they put on shiny dance outfits and scraped their brown hair up into very tight knots on their heads and went to what they called Modern Jazz classes. Then Disco classes followed on afterwards. Sometimes Tap classes followed Disco. But Disco was their best. And they had loads of silver cups in the sitting room cabinet to prove it. The house was forever pulsing with 'Boogie Wonderland' or 'D.I.S.C.O' or 'I Will Survive', and if you walked into the dining room without checking first you were likely to get a smack in the face from a twirling spangly stick, which was part of some of their routines.

They *were* good dancers, Eddie had to admit, but their singing was dreadful and nobody in their family seemed to have noticed. Auntie Kath was convinced that her twins were going to be hugely famous.

The other problem was that none of them seemed to have an embarrassment chip. For Eddie, practising a song-and-dance routine in a queue outside a tourist attraction was as appealing as doing naked handstands in the middle of school assembly. But the self-consciousness component in this family was missing. They just didn't think that constantly showing off to complete strangers, without ever being asked, was in any way odd. Being twelve, Eddie was an expert in embarrassment, which was why he was so surprised to find he'd been quietly singing his 'Bogey Wonderland' lyrics out loud. Oh no . . . it must be catching. He'd only been with them a week and already he was performing in public.

'Queue's moving!' said Auntie Kath and Kayleigh and Chanelle broke off from their gyrating and shimmied along the path instead. Eddie was hugely relieved that the queue was quite short. It had been a bad summer for tourism so far, with foot and mouth disease striking the country once more. Although the Wookey Hole caves, unlike attractions with animals, were open to the public, not many people were travelling far from home. Most of the people in this queue were likely to be locals, from Bristol or Bath maybe. Somerset wasn't an afflicted area, so people in the county could still travel through the countryside. Auntie Kath, Damon, Kayleigh, and Chanelle had been here at least twice before and were really more excited by the indoor play area, slot machines, and gift shop at the end of the tour than the caves themselves.

Eddie, though, was excited about the caves. He'd never been into real caves before. He lived in East Sussex, where the land was green and pretty and flat. No caves in East Sussex. This outing was the best thing that had happened since he had arrived this summer in the Mendip Hills to stay with his aunt and cousins. His mother had been very ill and now needed time alone with just his dad, so she could recover. Dad had asked his sister if she would take Eddie and she had said he could stay for the whole summer if need be. She hadn't wanted him to come, Eddie had since decided. He could tell this by the number of times she said the words 'Christian duty' to her various friends when they dropped by the house. It was her Christian duty to look after her nephew while poor Ellen was getting better. Her Christian duty to put up a camp bed for him in Damon's room. Her Christian duty to feed him and take him out with her own children. Auntie Kath was not unkind to him, but she made sure he was well aware of the cost of all the kindness he did get. All he had to do in return was be constantly grateful. It was exhausting.

'Thanks ever so much for taking me here today,' he said, as they walked into the opening of the caves where the guide was waiting for them in the cool underground air.

'That's quite all right, Edward,' said Auntie Kath. 'What kind of an aunt would I be if I didn't bring you along too?' Eddie smiled gratefully.

'Are we all in?' said the guide, a young man in a Wookey Hole fleece, carrying a torch. There was a murmur from the small group of about a dozen people standing in the wide cave opening. There was nobody else in the queue behind them.

'Good,' said the guide. 'Now—welcome to Wookey Hole, where a river flows from the underworld and pagan and Christian legends abound! Follow me into a world of witches and saints, of cave people and explorers, of divers and danger!'

Eddie looked around him and grinned. The air smelled of earth and metal and water and the roof of the cave seemed to reach down to him with its stubby stone stalactite fingers. *Or was that stalagmite?* he wondered, as they trooped down a dimly lit passageway after the guide. *How did you remember? Ummm . . . Stalactite . . . the c was for ceiling. And stalagmite, the g was for ground.* He thought . . . Anyway, they were stone icicles going up and down and it was really properly spooky.

After a bit more talk about the history of the

caves, the guide led them down some steps, hewn into the rock, and they arrived in the 'Witch's Kitchen': a larger chamber opening out around a subterranean river, its clear, glassy water lit from beneath the surface and glowing gold and green. The guide showed them a huge stalagmite which seemed to rear up out of the rock floor. Then he shone his torch onto a large misshapen rock, close to the water, said to be the petrified witch. Eddie wasn't convinced. It looked more like a deformed potato to him.

'She was cooking a child in her cauldron when she was sprinkled with holy water by a monk,' whispered the guide, who was obviously an out of work actor, thought Eddie. Chanelle and Kayleigh were fascinated by him and stood, gaping, hanging on his every dramatic word. Damon hadn't taken his earphones out and simply bopped along to a song only he could hear, his eyes idly roving the walls and ceiling and his mouth working tirelessly on a lump of bubblegum. He'd seen it before and wasn't impressed. He shoved Eddie back behind him, though, as they made their way on through another narrow passage.

'Oi!' complained Eddie, rubbing his chest where Damon's hard elbow had struck. Damon made an 'aww, poor baby' kind of face and then went on ahead.

'Nice chap, your cousin.' Eddie looked round,

surprised. He had thought he was the last person in the queue of visitors, but there was a man behind him. An old man. His hair was silvery white and his eyes, behind his spectacles, were grey and rather pink in the corners.

'Well . . . he's always like that,' said Eddie, as if it was an excuse. Which, of course, it wasn't. Damon was a thug. He was top in sports at school and liked to use his cousin's head as target practice for rugby, basketball, or football. Eddie had been woken up three times already this week with some kind of sports equipment bashing into his face. He was hoping his cousin would stop short of the ice hockey stick which stood in the corner of his bedroom. He *would* complain about the bruises to his aunt, but feared this would be seen as less than grateful. She was doing her Christian duty, after all. He complained to Damon, at the time, of course, and obviously badly wanted to get up and smack his cousin's face in, but this wasn't really a sensible option. Damon was a year older and several times harder than Eddie. He'd already broken the nose of a boy at school. Auntie Kath insisted it was only 'playing around', but you only had to look at Damon's block-like face to realize that 'playing around' with him was a very bad idea. Mostly, Eddie just stayed out of his way.

'You're not anything like him, are you?' said the strange man. 'Or the rest of them.'

'I hope not,' muttered Eddie, moving away after the tour party.

'You go your own way, don't you?' said the man, standing still as Eddie looked back at him. He realized the man was wearing a Wookey Hole staff fleece.

'Um . . . yeah,' said Eddie. He glanced back to the tour party which had nearly disappeared now around a bend in the cave passage. Without them the Witch's Kitchen looked better. More serious. Real.

'Well,' said the man. Eddie squinted at him, confused.

'Well what?' he asked.

The man smiled and pointed to his left. 'Your own way,' he said, smiling broadly and somehow *expectantly* at Eddie. Eddie followed the line of the man's finger and saw what looked like a small dark seam in the rock face of the cave. 'Move left a little and see,' said the man.

Eddie looked around him uneasily. Was this guy the staff weirdo? The one they had to employ on some government Employ This Weirdo initiative. The one who was never allowed a tour party of his own, for safety reasons. But still, he moved slightly to his left and then gasped as he saw that the line in the rock was not just a darker streak of limestone, but actually a gap. A gap that led somewhere.

'It's fine, you know. You will be safe,' smiled the man. 'They don't take people down here because some are too fat to get through. You're small and thin. You'll be fine. There are better chambers beyond. Here—you'll need this.' He handed Eddie a torch. Eddie took it and stepped towards the narrow, slanting gap. He was nervous. Unsure.

'I will wait for you here,' said the man. His smile was very calm, very steady. He looked at Eddic as if he had known him for a very long time. 'Mind your head and keep turning to your right. You should come back to the passageway of your own accord. Then we can catch up with the others.'

Eddie opened his mouth to ask why he was being given this special treatment. Then he closed it again. He should be very, very suspicious. An old guy offers you a secret passageway outing in a cave and you just shrug and *go*? Yeah, right! And yet . . . it was that smile. A smile that seemed to hold ages and ages of knowledge. Further up the passageway the voices of the main party were echoing back. He heard Kayleigh and Chanelle singing. They were obviously amused by the echo and going back into their act for the assembled party. Eddie shuddered, switched on the torch, and stepped into the gap in the rock.

Chapter 2

At first he thought the Wookey Weirdo might follow him, but the man did not. He just stood still, back in the Witch's Kitchen, and briskly flapped his hands at Eddie, encouraging him to go on.

With his heart thumping rather hard in his chest, Eddie swung the torch around and peered along the passageway. It slanted off to one side and a taller boy would have had to lean sideways with it as he walked on, but Eddie was quite small and could stand up straight. The limestone rock looked the same as in the previous cave—smooth and undulating, with more pale stalactites hanging above him. He couldn't see where the top of the cave roof was, because it just folded away from him on an angle, into the dark, but the slanted walls dripped with petrified minerals, like the fingers of a thousand aliens reaching down to him. He shivered and shone the torch ahead of him. The passageway went straight for a few metres and then veered to the left. Under his feet the floor was smooth and softly ribbed. He guessed this had once been the bed of another underground river. There were all kinds of waterways that threaded through this network of caves, apparently.

Eddie took a deep breath and stepped forward. His footsteps made little noise, as he was in soft-soled trainers, but his breathing seemed very loud to his own ears, slapping against the slant of the wall which was so close to his left temple. He could hear trickling and at one point his foot made a splashing noise as it fell. He shone his torch down and saw a small rivulet of water winding across the passageway and disappearing into a gap, low in the rock.

He went on. Around to the right the passageway widened a little and the headroom was higher. Still he could not see the roof of this sliver of cave, but more impressive stalactites were twisting down from above like melted wax candles. How far along was he now? How far from the others? He had better go round fast and get back to the Wookey Weirdo, or he'd be missed and would get into trouble. He quickened his step, aware of a low hissing noise. He reached a fork in the passageway. One path led off to the left and seemed to descend, while the other stayed flat and went right. Stay to the left, the man had said. He shrugged and followed the downward path, although it was narrower and less inviting than the right-hand path.

The path twisted abruptly further to the right and then pitched down at quite a steep angle. He caught hold of some outcrops of stalagmites to his sides as his trainers slid a little on the smooth floor. The hissing sound was louder and deeper now—it sounded muffled and echoey. In fact it was almost a roar. He moved on, feeling quite nervous. It was time he wound back to the main cave and found the man again. He'd been going for five minutes by now, surely? He examined his watch with the torch. Well—four minutes at any rate. Ah—there was a second switch on the torch, he noticed. As he stepped around another large outcrop of limestone sculpture, he pushed the button and extra light, pale blue, suddenly flooded out of the torch from further down its barrel. Ah! He realized it was a kind of lantern too, with a hanging strap at the holding end. He picked it up from the strap and held it high and then gasped at what it picked out. The ceiling was vaulted with beautifully dripping stone, curving up away from him in a concave dome. It felt like a cathedral. Off to one corner were some low smooth lumps of rock and just beyond them he could see movement—sparkling, glistening movement. Now he realized what the muffled hissing and roaring had been. He moved across and leaned over the rocks to see, in one corner of this immense chamber, a twisting, turning, tumbling, blue-black waterfall. Fine spray rose from it, scented with ancient minerals, settling across his nose and brow.

'Wow!' said Eddie, out loud. He held the lantern out, swinging, further across the waterfall which cascaded into view from a hole in the cave wall about two metres above his head and plunged into a shallow pool of smoothly worked limestone, maybe the size of a kid's garden paddling pool, before rushing away and disappearing into a convoluted chute of stone to some underworld he would never see. The anguished, frantic liquid sent up bubbles and gurgles which warbled just above the hiss and the roar. The roar seemed to be rising up from some way down in the rocky tunnel of water. Eddie shone the lantern as close to the pool's exit as he could reach and caught sight of a tangle of watery ribbons, wriggling endlessly, far below him.

'Wow!' he said again. 'Oh!' he gasped, as he dropped the light. There was a three second moment when he *might* have retrieved it as it spun across the surface of the shallow cauldron, sending light in a wild, dancing arc through the water. But after two shocked blinks of an eye it had upended, sending a beam of blue-white up through the waterfall above it, before vanishing down the chute of water. There were two more glimpses of man-made light and then a cracking noise and a second later Eddie was surrounded by the blackest dark he had ever known.

He gulped and whimpered, 'Oh no!' as he sank down against the low rock. His eyes opened wider. He could *feel* his pupils *straining* for light. Some light. *Any* light. Just one tiny pinprick of light. There was none. He turned his head in the direction he *thought* he had come into the cave from. Surely some light from the Witch's Kitchen could reach here . . . eventually. As soon as his eyes had adjusted, the slightest lightening of black to grey would show him where to go.

He sat and waited, his heart now hammering with fright and his breath coming out hard and ragged. After what must have been more than a minute, his eyes still felt as if they were sheathed in thick black velvet. Whether they were open or closed, the view of total blackness was unchanged.

'OK, OK, Eddie . . . *think*!' he murmured, loud enough to hear himself above the water noise. '*Think*. The man knows where you've gone. In a few minutes, when you don't come back, he'll come for you. Just

14

wait. There will be a torch flashing in here, any time. Any time now.'

After another minute or more—he couldn't see his watch so he didn't know—he repeated, 'Any time now.'

He stood up, shakily, and began to move away from the sound of the waterfall. He was fairly sure that the entrance into the bigger cave had been opposite the waterfall. So he should reach it soon. His hands out in front of him, he shuffled forward, feeling through the air for the wall of the cave. Once he had the wall, he would work along it, moving away from the waterfall noise. And this would take him to the passage out of here. Wouldn't it?

'Think,' he said again, out loud, and his voice sounded high and scared. 'Was there any other way leading out of this cave? Or j-just the way you came in?' If there was another way leading on from the cave—or maybe even *another*—then he could wander off down a passageway he hadn't been through yet—and get even more lost. But no—he had to keep going right, the man had said. Or was it left? Left or right? Which? He couldn't remember. Eddie felt real panic unwind its tentacles in the pit of his stomach. Like a cold squid inside him, it began to wake up and stretch towards his chest and throat. No! He stopped and

15

breathed as evenly as he could. Cool. Calm. No panic. The man would come . . . would find him as he was making his way back probably.

He shuffled forward again, arms still outstretched, and then something struck him hard, right in the middle of the forehead. Blue and red stars suddenly bloomed across his vision, like a small firework display—the only light he could filter into his brain in this pitilessly dark place. But he knew it was just inside his own head. He felt dizzy as he lifted his hand to his brow. It was sticky. He was bleeding. A low hanging stalactite had found him. More dizziness assailed him. He knew he should get his head down or he might faint. He crouched down, feeling the smooth ripples of the limestone beneath his palms, and leaned his head down between his knees. Very soon, in maybe a minute or so, when his head had cleared, he was going to have to start shouting for help. He didn't want to. Actually hearing himself cry out for aid would make this whole thing very, very real. Until then, it was manageable. But once it was real, he didn't know how he would cope.

They must have missed him by now. Auntie Kath and the twins and Damon must have retraced their steps. And surely they would ask the Wookey Weirdo if he'd seen him and he would admit what had happened and come in after him. Or (now the panic tentacles writhed harder against the inside of his throat) maybe he wouldn't. Maybe this was what he did. He liked to send kids off alone to get lost and die in caves. And nobody would ever know what he'd done . . . Not until it was far, far too late.

Eddie hitched in a breath which sounded like a sob and lifted his head. He was going to shout for help now. He was going to do it. He opened his mouth to yell—but instead he gasped out in shock.

Someone had just taken hold of his hand.

Chapter 3

'Who's that?' he shrieked, a second later. The fingers were cool and smooth and dry, grasping his right hand and encouraging him to sit up.

'Shhh,' said a voice. 'Be still. Be calm. You're injured.'

'Wha-what?' He was waggling his head from side to side, desperate to see the source of this voice. It was a young, sweet voice. Most definitely not the Wookey Weirdo. It sounded like a girl.

'Who are you? What's going on? How come you can *see* me?'

'Oh!' exclaimed the voice. 'Of course. I forgot. Here.' There was a scratching sound and suddenly a small pale glow effused into his vision. His starved eyes seemed to drink it greedily in, so that at first the light was all he could see.

'Is that better?' said the girl. For a girl it was. After a few seconds he could see her features picked out in the gloom. She was smiling. He thought she was about his age—maybe slightly younger. Her eyes were large and almost luminous in a rather elf-like face. Her smile was wide and curious and her pale hair hung far below her shoulders. He saw that she was wearing what looked like a thin vest top and some trousers. She raised her light to his face and he blinked. She touched his brow gently.

'It's all right. Only a little cut. It's already stopped bleeding.'

'Who are you?' breathed Eddie. 'Did—did the weirdo guy send you in to get me?'

'Weirdo guy?' she repeated, squinting at him across the glow of light, which seemed to waver and gently pulse. 'Oh!' Laughter suddenly lit up her features and danced around the chamber, chasing all the dank, dark fear right out of it. 'Oh—you must mean Stan! I will have to tell him that one!' She laughed some more.

'Look—do you, I dunno, work here or something? Or are you someone's kid? Some staff member's daughter?'

'Come on,' she said, getting to her feet and pulling him up. 'You're going to be late back and you'll get into trouble. You took the wrong turning, silly. I'll take you back now. Follow me. Mind your head.'

Ducking down under another low stalactite, Eddie stumbled along after his strange guide, who was still holding tight to his hand. He did not want to let go, even if she was a girl. In any other circumstances it would have been highly embarrassing, but there was no way he wanted to be left alone in the blackness again. They seemed to turn several times, left *and* right. And then he saw the odd, slanted passageway ahead of them and a few diamonds of light hitting a distant wall of rock. The light from the Witch's Kitchen! He puffed out a loud sigh of relief.

'You can go on from here,' said the girl. In the better light he saw that she was slight and smaller than him by two or three inches. Her hair looked almost white and her eyes were a pale silvery-lilac colour.

'Aren't you coming too?' he asked. 'Shouldn't we both be getting back?'

She smiled and shook her head, before tilting it to one side and, oddly, holding out her hand. 'My name is Gwerren,' she said. 'It's nice to meet you, Eddie.' He shook her hand, unable to think of what to say. Then she said, 'See you again one day, maybe,' and blinked away into the dark.

Eddie almost panicked again. She had switched off her light thing and just . . . gone. And then he saw the dim glow reaching along the passage from the Witch's

Kitchen and began to make his way to it. How did that girl move around in the dark? What was *that* about? And where had she run off to?

A minute later he emerged, blinking, into the golden light of the Witch's Kitchen. The Wookey Weirdo—or Stan, as the girl had called him—was still waiting and still smiling.

'Have they been searching for me?' he demanded, looking around for panicky relatives, but Stan shook his head. He inclined it towards the path that Auntie Kath and Damon and the twins had gone along some time before and Eddie gaped in amazement as he heard the last few bars of 'Boogie Wonderland' being murdered by his cousins. 'They didn't even notice I was gone?' He gave an astonished chuckle.

'Time moves strangely in here,' said Stan. 'Better catch them up now. Here—take this with you.' He handed Eddie a leaflet—some kind of special offer thing for this and other attractions in the area.

'Er . . . thanks, Stan.' Eddie pushed it into his pocket and moved along the passage. 'And thanks for letting me see the waterfall . . . Sorry—I lost your torch. I'd better move on now.'

'Any time, Eddie, any time,' smiled Stan. 'Don't forget to look at your leaflet. Goodbye.'

Eddie ran up the passageway just in time to hear

21

a ripple of applause for 'Boogie Wonderland'. What a freaky, freaky day. The secret passage, the cave, the waterfall, that *girl*! And how could she see him when he couldn't see her? Freaky!

And one more thing, he thought, as he reached the party and joined in with making impressed noises about the twins' performance, just behind his aunt—how did Stan and that girl know his name?

Chapter 4

'Uncle Wilf! Look what I brought you back from Wookey Hole!' Eddie peered around the door of Uncle Wilf's room, clutching a paper bag. Uncle Wilf was in his chair, straining to see his little TV as usual. He looked up and smiled at Eddie, who wasn't actually his nephew; just the son of his nephew's wife's brother. Which wasn't a proper nephew. It didn't matter though. Wilf *felt* like Eddie's uncle, so that's what he called him.

'Come in, son,' said Uncle Wilf, patting the stool next to him. 'Come and take my mind off my joints and this good-for-nothing box of tricks!' Eddie went over to the little portable TV and fiddled with its indoor aerial. The screen swarmed with dots, enveloping a 1990s repeat of *Countdown*, and its inbuilt speaker hissed and coughed and occasionally someone said, 'Can I have a consonant please, Carol?' It was a rubbish

TV and having an indoor aerial was almost totally useless. They were in a deep cleft of the Mendip Hills, for goodness' sake. You'd struggle to get a signal even if the broadcasting mast was just up the road in Cheddar.

'Why can't Auntie connect you up to Sky?' he asked, not for the first time. The rest of the family got hundreds of perfectly clear channels from satellite TV in the lounge, the kitchen, and even in Damon's bedroom, but poor Uncle Wilf had to make do with the three and a half channels that could still be picked up with an aerial. And they wouldn't be available for much longer. Soon everything would be digital and there would be nothing to watch but dirty snow.

'Better start listening to the radio,' sighed Eddie, giving the TV a hard whack on its side, which didn't improve anything. 'Or come into the lounge with the rest of us.'

Uncle Wilf snorted and Eddie smiled and rubbed his hand through his messy red hair. He knew why Uncle Wilf didn't want to sit and watch TV in the lounge. The same reason *he* didn't. For one thing, his cousins and their mother seemed to be incapable of just watching something. They had to give a non-stop running commentary. 'Oh—she really shouldn't have worn that,' his aunt would opine, goggling at some reality TV show. 'That really does nothing for her at all! *Look* at that neckline! Trollop! And if those are real, I'm the queen!'

'Get it! Get it! Get it *in*! OOOH! You loser!' was Damon's usual line of commentary. He viewed sport a lot, although it seemed to cause him untold distress. Nobody ever did the right thing. Unless they won, of course. And then it was only because of the advice they got from Damon's corner of the sofa.

The twins just wittered and giggled and sang across whatever was happening, unless it featured kittens or puppies, in which case the room rang to the sound of their cries of adoration and longing.

Their father, Eddie's uncle John, was away on long business trips, so Eddie didn't yet know what kind of vocal accompaniment *he* would offer up, during TV time. Maybe he would just grunt every six seconds. Or whistle through his teeth.

The kind of TV they liked wasn't what he liked, anyway. He liked natural history and wildlife and survival type shows, but he didn't think this family even paid for those channels and they rarely bothered with BBC.

Consequently, Eddie spent quite a lot of time at his cousins' home with Uncle Wilf. A twelve-year-old boy and a man in his eighties was an odd pairing but it seemed to work.

Eddie gave up on the TV and handed Uncle Wilf the paper bag instead. Inside was a bar of fudge and a postcard showing scenes of the caves. 'Aaah,' said Uncle Wilf, unwrapping the bar of fudge with enthusiasm. 'Aaaaah,' he said, more thoughtfully, as he saw the postcard. 'The caves, was it? Did you like them?'

'Like them? I *love* them!' said Eddie, perching on the old leather stool next to Uncle Wilf's chair. 'We went all round, through this really low, flat cave, like—I dunno—like the inside of a sherbet saucer—you had to duck down—and then these incredibly tall thin ones with stalactites hanging down like spears and then over the river on metal catwalks and . . . ' He noticed that Uncle Wilf was watching him, chewing on his fudge and nodding, smiling. He wondered whether to tell him about the weird man called Stan and getting lost and the strange girl . . . but worried that it might sound as if he was making up stories. He shivered as he thought of it. It had been really scary, but kind of exciting too. The rest of the tour had been great, but his mind had kept slithering away back to that secret cave and the waterfall and his lost torch and the girl.

'Ooooh,' Auntie Kath had shuddered, as the guide told them about the furthest reaches of the cave divers' discoveries. The caves ran on and on, deeper and deeper, with who knows how large a network of subterranean rivers. The potholers and cavers who explored them were always hoping for another breakthrough—another magical underground discovery. 'I wouldn't fancy that much,' grimaced Auntie Kath. 'Potholing? Ugh. Like a worm. It's not natural to go burrowing down into the earth like that.'

'But if they hadn't done it, we would never have been able to see this,' Eddie had pointed out, looking down from the metal catwalk they were crossing at the eerily silent river that flowed far below them, picked out with pools of blue-green electric lighting which those potholers and cave divers must have installed.

His aunt sniffed. She did that whenever anyone said something sensible which she chose not to acknowledge. 'Gives me the creeps,' she muttered, a few seconds later.

'Can we hurry up and get to the play area?' whined Kayleigh. 'This is taking for*ever*!'

At the last cave on the tour they had squeezed past the guide and the rest of the party and made their own way ahead to the play area, not interested in hearing the final part of the talk. Eddie had not followed them. He'd wanted to stay in the caves for as long as he could. Eventually, when the guide came back in to check on him, he'd had to leave the caves and walk down through the valley alongside the river Axe, past some incongruous dinosaur models and into the museum and amusements area, where he found the others. The twins were climbing around in the play arena, squeaking, while Damon angrily thumped the glass of an old-fashioned arcade game. Auntie Kath sat on a bench, amid some ketchup-splashed fast food wrappings, and watched her daughters. She had handed Eddie a cold burger in a carton. 'Thought you were never coming,' she said, never taking her eyes off the play arena.

He'd wanted to loop around and do the tour a second time.

Eddie shivered again, remembering the torch, the waterfall, the girl.

'It's cold enough to freeze the nicknacks off a newt in here,' commented Uncle Wilf, watching him. He wasn't wrong. Uncle Wilf's 'room' was actually the garage. A side door from the house led into it and they'd laid a thin carpet down on the concrete floor, painted the breezeblocks magnolia, and put in a bed, an armchair, and a few other sticks of elderly furniture from Uncle Wilf's old house. Two years ago, getting infirm with his arthritis, Uncle Wilf had sold his house, put all the money into a bank account and moved in with his niece so she could care for him 'as her Christian duty'. It was Auntie Kath's idea and it had made sense at the time, he'd told Eddie.

They spent some of his money putting a toilet and shower room in at the back end of the garage. Auntie Kath called it an 'en suite' but that was rather a grand name for just a very basic toilet and a tiny basin and a feeble shower which rarely got above luke-warm. Eddie knew this, because he had used it, with Uncle Wilf's permission, when Damon had been hogging the shower room in the main house and the twins had bagged the bathroom for Disco Championship preparation. Poor Uncle Wilf's shower was like being dribbled on by a toddler with a slight temperature. No wonder he always longed for a hot bath. Hot, steamy water was the only thing that eased the aches in his gnarled old fingers. But he rarely got one. He needed help getting in and out of it, and Auntie Kath didn't often feel that her Christian duty could stretch that far.

'Shall I get you a hot water bottle?' asked Eddie, noticing that Uncle Wilf's knuckles looked more swollen than usual.

'No, no, don't you bother yourself; would you mind?'

Eddie ran back into the house and up to the bathroom where the water bottles were kept. He filled one with water as hot as he could get it and then took it back.

'You tell Uncle Wilf *not* to take that into bed with him,' warned Auntie Kath as he passed her in the kitchen. 'If it bursts it'll ruin the mattress. And we can't afford to get him another one. He is *such* an expense!'

Eddie closed the door from the kitchen into Uncle Wilf's garage and the old man grinned at him. 'It's all right, son. I heard. Wouldn't want to cost anyone any more money, would I?'

'But,' said Eddie, sitting back down on the leather footstool and wrinkling his brow, 'what about all the money in your bank account—that you got for selling your house?'

'Oh, that's all gone,' sighed Uncle Wilf.

'Gone? How much was it?'

'Oh, I forget. Seventy or eighty.'

'Thousand?'

He nodded and pulled the hot water bottle to his belly, against the old brown wool cardigan which had seen better days. He sighed with relief as he pressed his palms against it. 'Thaaaaat's better. Thanks, Eddie.'

'You mean to say that you've spent eighty thousand pounds in two years?' Eddie gasped.

'Cost of living is very high,' muttered Uncle Wilf. 'Your aunt has to keep me fed and watered and get the doctor round and—well—the shower and all that . . . '

Eddie looked around him at the cold, damp room that was Uncle Wilf's home. There wasn't even a proper window in it; just a narrow skylight, high on the wall. The front of the room, which would have had a window in it, had it *been* a proper room, was the garage door. A gas canister heater stood by it and was switched on from time to time through the day. Auntie Kath switched it off at night to save fuel, while Uncle Wilf was in bed. The room was always either cold and damp or clammy and fuggy. Condensation permanently steamed up the skylight.

Eddie was twelve. He didn't know a lot about money and how far it went, but he was quite certain that the toilet and shower could not have cost more than a few thousand pounds to put in. And how much could it cost to feed Uncle Wilf? And didn't doctors come and visit free of charge?

'How can eighty thousand pounds have been spent—in two years?' he said, again.

Uncle Wilf laughed, staring down at his hands, and Eddie felt his embarrassment. 'A fool and his money are soon parted,' he mumbled. 'Still, if I live for a good many more years, your aunt will have earned it, won't she?' He chuckled.

Eddie didn't say anything more about the money. He was shocked but not actually that surprised. His aunt's kindnesses were always carefully measured. Now he remembered his dad offering her money for his keep while he was there. He didn't remember how much, but he didn't remember her turning it down, either.

'Tell me about the old days,' he said, to take their minds to a brighter subject.

'You don't want to hear about the old days from an old codger like me, do you? Really? Well, all right then, if you like,' said Uncle Wilf. 'Well now, the Mendips are like a world apart from anywhere else I've ever been. And I've been all over the world, did you know that? When I was in the army. A long, long time ago. Of course, it was no holiday. You didn't send picture postcards back from where I went . . . '

Uncle Wilf had fought in the Second World War. He'd seen some pretty nasty things, even before he ended up as a prisoner of war. Some of them he told Eddie about. Some of them he didn't. Eddie could tell that the things he did not talk about were much, much worse than the things he did. Wilf had never married. He had been in love though,

Eddie knew, although he didn't talk about that very much at all. 'People laughed,' was all he said on that score. 'People always laugh at what they don't understand.'

When he had finished this story—about his time in North Africa and how he'd got to know the local children near the camp and taught them silly English songs—Uncle Wilf lapsed into silence, his eyes distant and dreamy. 'That was another lifetime,' he said. 'Another world.' The water in the rubber bottle glopped and gurgled as he pressed his fingers into it. They looked a little less swollen.

'Eddie—tea's ready. Come along,' called his aunt, opening the door. 'Leave Uncle Wilf alone, now. We don't want him getting tired out, do we?'

'Don't we?' muttered Uncle Wilf in a low voice.

'I'll see you later,' said Eddie. 'I'll come in to say goodnight.'

At the table there were plates of chips and peas and fishfingers. Damon was squeezing an enormous puddle of ketchup onto the side of his plate. The twins had already decorated their chips with many scarlet splashes. By the time the bottle came to Eddie there was hardly any sauce left in it. He squeezed it and it made a rude noise, squirting out a fine red rosette. He sighed and gave up. He took a sip of his lemonade and tried not to wince. Auntie Kath always bought diet drinks, as part of her endless battle against the stodginess around her middle. His cousins were used to the nasty chemical aftertaste, but he wasn't. His mum hated him drinking chemicals and would instead put fizzy mineral water and fresh fruit juice together—or even let him have proper lemonade or cola from time to time. 'Sugar in moderation is fine,' she'd say. 'We can mend your teeth if need be—but I'm not so sure about your brain.' She was convinced that artificial sweeteners damaged your brain. Observing Damon and the twins, he thought she might well be right. Thinking about her gave Eddie a pang of homesickness. How many more weeks did he have to be here? How could he ever survive? A wave of sadness rolled over him. He wished and wished he could go home. He felt like an alien here. When would Mum be well enough for him to go back? Was she really going to be OK?

'Ooooh, loooook! Little Eddie-weddy's cryin'!'

Eddie looked up, blinking back tears that were *almost* at his eyes. Damon yaffed up and down on a mouthful of chips and fish finger, displaying the progress his teeth were making with every munch. He didn't seem to know about breathing through his nose and keeping his mouth shut while eating. He was noisy and greedy and would often nick food off other people's plates when he'd finished his own. The twins habitually ate with one arm shielding their meal.

'I'm *not* crying!' said Eddie. He speared a chip and tried to get a bit of the dregs of ketchup on it. 'I was just . . . thinking.'

'What about? Your *mummy*?'

'Yes,' said Eddie. 'She has been ill, you know.'

'That's what she told *you*,' said Damon, shovelling more food in. 'But I think they made it up, your mum and dad, so they could get shot of you for a few weeks. Who'd want a drippy little dipstick like *you* around all the time?'

Eddie felt rage searing through his chest. His mother had been *so* ill they had thought she might die. He still wasn't certain that she would ever get properly well.

His cousin was laughing now. 'They're probably having loads of parties and schtuff.' Damon spattered the edge of Eddie's plate with bits of semi-chewed chip. 'Getting all vere mates round for danshin' and schtuff.' The twins let off identical shrill giggles. Eddie put down his knife and fork and found his hands were balled into fists.

'I bet they're doin' the Eddie's Gone Boogie! *Yeah! Eddie's gone! Let's all have some fun! Yeah! Eddie's gone! Let's all have some fun!*' He began to dance about in his seat and the twins joined in, getting up and going into one of their disco routines while chanting along. *Yeah! Eddie's gone! Let's all have some fun!* Damon gurned across the table at him, a dribble of ketchup rolling down his chin.

Eddie stood up, picked up his food-laden plate and smacked it into his cousin's face.

Chapter 5

'Really, Eddie, after all we've done to make you feel at home here,' sighed Auntie Kath, sponging some fish and breadcrumbs off Damon's face.

Eddie said nothing. His hands were tight fists still as he stood by the fridge.

'He's a nutter! That's what he is!' snarled Damon. 'Just gets up and shoves his plate in my face, out of nowhere! What's that all about, eh? He's a nutter.'

'You were saying stuff about my mum!' muttered Eddie.

'We was just 'avin a laugh! A joke!' Damon rolled his eyes and shrugged at his sisters who were staring at the scene and biting their lower lips, enjoying the drama. Damon's shriek of rage when he got a fish finger in one eye and a pea up a nostril, had brought Auntie Kath running. If she'd been a few seconds later

Eddie would probably have a broken nose, so he supposed he was lucky, really.

'Eddie, you must try to be a bit less sensitive,' advised his aunt. 'I know you're an only child and it's hard for you, but all children tease each other. There's no need to go throwing good food around.'

'Sorry, Auntie,' said Eddie, because he didn't want her to think he didn't appreciate the food. He did.

'Well anyway, it's time to get ready, so hurry upstairs and get changed,' she said, propelling Damon towards the foot of the stairs and waving at Eddie to follow. Kayleigh and Chanelle began to give off high-pitched squeaks, like excited guinea pigs, so Eddie guessed they were all going off to another disco championship event. Damon groaning on the stairs ahead of him confirmed his guess. It was the one thing he and his cousin agreed on. Not *another* disco thing.

As Eddie changed into some cleaner clothes, pulling them out of the carrier bag under his low camp bed, Damon ignored his mother's request to get changed and instead began some basketball practice. The hoop and net was attached to the wall on the far side of the room from his cabin bed, and just because it was right over Eddie's bed was no reason for Damon not to use it. Day and night. In fact that was the way Eddie usually woke up. With the thud and rattle of the basketball hoop and then a hard bash of a leather basketball on his chest or shoulder or face. He had put his pillow end as far from the hoop as he could, and now it was jammed up against a radiator which slammed out loads of heat all night (the house was always overheated, apart from in Uncle Wilf's bit). He had a choice of baked head or bashed head. The baked head won, just. Eddie didn't get much sleep—which was probably why he'd got all emotional over his tea.

As he prepared to bundle his dirty clothes into the laundry, Eddie heard a crackle. He retrieved something from the jeans pocket. It was the Wookey Hole leaflet and . . . yes . . . something else folded into it. This was what that bloke Stan had given him. Some kind of special offer. He expected it to be one of those Child-Goes-Free-With-Paying-Adult-type things, but it wasn't. Pausing over the laundry basket in the bathroom, Eddie unfolded the square bit of paper. It was yellow and shiny, with the Witch of Wookey cartoon at the top, and below that some black lettering read:

WOOKEY HOLE—FULL FREE ACCESS
FOR JULY & AUGUST

Underneath this was a printed row of dots, and handwritten on it in blue ink was his name:

Below this were the words **AUTHORIZED BY** and a scrawly signature that he could not read.

Eddie gaped at the piece of paper. For one thing, how *had* that Wookey guy known his name? He thought for a moment . . . he supposed Auntie Kath might have written down all their names at the ticket booth . . . maybe for a . . . a competition or something. Win a holiday or get money off or something. Yes. Auntie Kath never turned down the chance of something free. And he must have won it and . . .

But it was still weird. Nevertheless, if it was real (and it did look real—on proper shiny paper) this meant he could go back to the caves! Any time at all this summer! On his own!

Eddie grinned and put the bit of paper carefully into his trouser pocket. He did not intend to share his good news with his cousins or his aunt. For a start, Auntie Kath would probably phone up the place and demand that they *all* won a free ticket. And if they said yes, he'd have to put up with the rest of them trailing in and out with him; although it would only be for the play area, he guessed. The amusement arcade and the play area were quite good—but they were *nothing* compared to the caves! The caves were just

amazing and he wanted to go back—on his own—
and take the tour again without Kayleigh and Chanelle
squeaking out 'D.I.S.C.O.', Auntie Kath going on about
how dark and cold it was, and Damon hitting his head
on a stalactite because he was playing his Nintendo
DS. How brilliant! Maybe, if he went really early, he
might be the *only one* on a tour! Would they still run
a tour if it was just him?

'Come along, you boys!' called up his aunt,
breaking into his excited planning. 'Time to go.'

Ah, thought Eddie, as he climbed into the back
of the shiny blue people mover, as far from Damon
as he could manage (it was a seven seater and brand
new only last year), but how am I going to get there?
He tried to remember the route they had taken, weaving
along the hairpin roads between the plunging hills. It
had taken about ten or fifteen minutes, he thought, to
reach the caves. So he guessed he'd be able to walk
there in forty-five maybe? It wouldn't be an easy walk,
though. Some of the roads were narrow and winding
and had no pavements, cutting through the tight gorges
of the Mendip hills. Even so—it would be worth the
risk. He had a free pass for the whole summer! He
was definitely going to use it.

'What are you grinning about, ginger nut?'
sneered Damon, leaning over the back of his seat and

41

staring at Eddie. Eddie thought about his free pass and grinned some more. 'Oh . . . just looking forward to a fantastic evening of disco,' he said.

She is D—disgusting
She is I—irritating
She is S—super stupid
She is C—constipated
She is O—ooooo—ooo!

Making up alternative words to the songs helped only slightly. The town hall was blinging with disco-ball beams, all skidding around the walls and ceilings, while troupes of little girls did their funky disco thing on the small stage. Chanelle and Kayleigh were in the centre, twirling batons with shiny red streamers hanging off them. They were wearing stretchy red outfits which hugged their rather square bodies and were adorned with random sequins, lovingly sewn on by Auntie Kath. Their ponytails were pulled so tight Eddie was sure their ears had risen a couple of centimetres higher and their glitter-lined eyes lifted at the corners like Siamese cats.

The dancing, he had to admit, was not that bad. Even if you weren't into disco. And he was definitely *not* into disco. You could see that they were pretty good at it. They could kick their legs higher than his head and the baton twirling was very expert. With both of them at it full pelt, they looked like a red spangly twin-rotored helicopter about to take off.

No, what made it really dreadful was that one of the dads ran a sound system hire company and had kitted out the main performers with microphones which could be attached to their sparkly heads like hands-free telephone kits. So every bump and breath and gasp of their routines was now playing out through the surround-sound speakers, along with their truly appalling attempts to sing like fully grown divas.

'D-I-S-C-O!' squeaked his cousins as they gyrated across the stage. 'D-I-S-C-OOOOOOH!' The number crashed to its finish and there was wild applause, contained only by the opening bars of yet another seventies classic.

Chanelle stepped up to the spotlight and began to sing.

'First I was afraid . . . '

' . . . I was mummified,' sang out Eddie, in his own head—an instant and effective protection against the horrors to come. 'Kept feeling like I was all bandaged down my right-hand side. But then I spent so many nights remembering you look like King Kong, and I grew strong—'cause girls with that much hair are wrong.'

On stage Chanelle clutched her heart and wailed, 'But now you're back! From outer space!'

'I just walked in to find you stuffing all my cheese strings in your face,' Eddie sang on, in his head, eyes tightly closed to avoid watching his cousin's bizarrely contorted features as she grappled unsuccessfully with the notes, in a completely different key to the backing track.

'I should have changed my stupid socks, I should have thrown you in the sea,' he persisted, desperately. 'If I'd've known for just one second you would scoff my Dairylea . . . '

It was no good. The music was too loud. He couldn't block it out. It was just awful and even the mothers in the audience were twitching and wincing as Chanelle, emoting like a reality TV star, got to the slowed down, dramatic 'Come—on—now—GO!' bit.

Eddie took her advice and walked out the door.

Outside the evening air was cool. It drifted across his face like a soothing hand and the thumping disco bass line began to retreat as he wandered across the small car park of the town hall and stared up at the high dark horizon of the hills. It was a clear night with an almost full moon low in the sky and a scattering of stars beginning to pinprick into view. Beautiful. The real glitter deal. He began to relax, sitting on the top of the low wall of the car park below a sign which read 'DANCE ALL OVER THE WORLD', giving details of yet another dancing event later that month. He leaned his back against it and let his eyes roam the hills, making out two or three dots of light moving down. Walkers returning late from the hills, he guessed. Suddenly Eddie stood up. Of course! There were many, many pathways over the Mendips. Walkers came from far and wide to trek around these parts. So there was almost certainly a route over the hills which would take him to Wookey Hole caves! All he needed to do was get one of those walkers' maps which showed you all the footpaths—and he could get there!

He wondered if Auntie Kath would let him, though. Maybe if he convinced her he was off bird watching or something, she might let him go out on his own. They knew he liked wildlife and he *had* got his binoculars with him, so he might be able to convince her. Eddie shivered with excitement. A couple of hours ago he had been gloomily eating fish fingers, dreading a whole summer in this place. But now—with his free pass to Wookey Hole caves and the chance to trek over to them alone—he was filled with fantastic anticipation.

Maybe, he thought, I will survive.

Chapter 6

The house which Eddie was required to call home for the summer was on the outskirts of Wells. It was very boxy and had those odd pillar things on either side of the door to make it look as if the house might, at first glance, be a Greek temple, rather than a detached three bedroom home, built in the 1980s. The windows had that leaded effect, in that they weren't leaded at all, but had criss-cross strips on the double glazing to make them look almost as if they were. It was a kind of ancient Greek Georgian farm style town house. All veneer and effect and quite out of keeping with the older houses built from local limestone, which were soft grey, sometimes with a reddish tinge.

Eddie left it early the next morning, with his walking boots on and his backpack over his shoulder. In his jeans pocket a banknote was folded—part of his precious holiday money which Dad had given him just before he'd driven away two weeks ago. Eddie was really glad he hadn't spent it. He needed to buy the map and he didn't know how much it would cost.

Getting out had been easier than he had expected. Rather than trying to ask nicely if he could be let out alone, Eddie decided to use what his mum would call 'reverse psychology'—which meant saying or doing the opposite of what you actually wanted, in order to get what you actually wanted. So at breakfast, while Chanelle and Kayleigh licked chocolate spread off their toast and Damon poured half a box of Coco Pops down his throat, Eddie said: 'I was thinking about going out bird spotting this morning. Want to come, Damon?'

Damon was so shocked he inhaled some Coco Pops. Auntie Kath had to thump him hard on the back and even then he was purple in the face and going 'Uuuuuurrrrgh . . . uuuuuurrrrgggghhhh,' until Eddie got up and joined in the thumping. He thumped his cousin's back very hard, even *after* he'd begun to breathe again.

'Shall I take that as a no, then, Day?' he smiled, innocently, as Damon turned round to shove him away and gurgle angrily at him.

'What? Go out lookin' at robins and sparrows and newts—with *you*?' he snorted.

47

'Well, maybe not the newts,' murmured Eddie, sitting back down to his toast. 'They'll have flown south for the summer.' Damon didn't blink. 'How about you two?' Eddie said brightly to the twins. They giggled and pulled faces. 'You not into birds, then?'

'Well—duur!' replied Chanelle, rolling her eyes. 'Like, totally—naaat!' (She watched a lot of Disney Channel, remembered Eddie.)

'You'd best go off on your own, dear,' said Auntie Kath, from the sink and Eddie had to shrug and sigh 'OK, then' and try *not* to leap up and punch the air for joy. Fantastic! He coughed and thought fast.

'Actually, I did say to my dad that I would try to do my school project on British birds and wildlife, while I was here. So . . . so maybe I should just get on with that over the next few days. Anyone who wants to join in can . . . if they want.'

The twins made noises like bottles of fizzy drink being opened after a shake up. Damon just yaffed Coco Pops and let his mouth hang open while he glared at his cousin.

'So—no takers? Well, I guess I'll just have to manage on my own, then.'

'Yes, you do your project, love,' said Auntie Kath, putting the kettle on to boil. 'You can take a packed lunch if you like. Just make sure you're home for tea.'

48

Now, just half an hour later, he was free! He could not believe how easy it had been. His aunt had even given him sandwiches and a flask of squash—and a notepad and some felt-tipped pens for drawing, which he'd put into his backpack along with his binoculars, a light fleece, a torch from the under-stairs cupboard and a handbook of British birds. They didn't have a decent map though, so he would need to buy his own. At the post office and general stores he found what he was looking for quickly. Lots of walkers came to the area and all shops kept a good stock of local maps and guides. He chose an Explorer map with great detail—even individual buildings were marked on it, along with footpaths and many wavy lines and figures to inform the map reader just how steep the hills were around here (if they hadn't already worked it out just by looking).

'Off on a trek, love?' said the nice lady at the shop, who liked him for his polite manner. He nodded. 'Have you got everything you need?' she went on. 'Food, drink, extra layers in case it gets cold?'

'Yup,' said Eddie, shouldering his bag.

'Well, just you mind how you go now,' she advised, patting his hair. 'There are still potholes and drops in the hills that aren't always on these maps. And don't you go leaning over the edge of the gorges.

Don't want to have to be getting cave rescue out after you, do we?'

Eddie grinned and went on his way, warmed by her concern. The new map crackled waxily between his fingers—and it had only cost him half his money. He made for the nearest footpath up into the hills. He would get a little way up, where he could still see the road, and then he would consult the map and work out his exact route across the hills.

The climb was steep, and he was puffing and hot after five minutes. It felt good. Silver birch, hazel, and holly trees grew, tall and slender, along the path, reaching high for the maximum sunlight. Birdsong and some distant cows mooing were all that he could hear alongside his own breathing and the crackle of the map in his hand. As he climbed higher the trees gave way to tall shrubs and thickets and then to tussocks of wild flowers or weeds hugging the dry stone walls which marked the boundaries between rolling meadows. He was surrounded by farmland: a green quilt spreading out in all directions, stitched with farm buildings and bridle paths. Low puddles of vegetation lay here and there, where the earth seemed to abruptly sink. Some of these hid potholes—vertical rock chimneys which could reach hundreds of feet down into the earth and even connect with caves. Many had been found and explored and mapped, but nobody knew how many there really were. Only last summer a new one had been unearthed on the upper slopes of a nearby gorge, hidden for centuries by fallen trees and full of Neolithic remains.

Eddie stepped to one side of the pathway to let two horses and their riders pass. 'Morning. Thank you,' said one of the riders, nodding his head at Eddie as they clopped heavily by. He resumed his trek. According to the map, he was about a third of the way across the hills towards the Wookey Hole caves, and should be able to enter the valley where the caves lay to the north, meeting the steep walkway as it rose to the main gate. He checked his pocket again for his pass and found it safely there.

Three more riders passed him over the next half hour and high above him a pair of buzzards rode the warm thermals of the summer morning. He got out his binoculars and followed them for a while, noting the white markings under their wings, before they flew west and out of his view. Moving on, he arrived at steeper terrain and knew he was at the head of the gorge that led down to the north end of the caves. His heart's drumbeat quickened. He was going to do it. He was going to achieve what he had set out to achieve.

The smell changed from warm sweet grass to cool earthy slope as he descended to the line of trees and tangled undergrowth which clung to the steep sides of the gorge. Below him a narrow pathway, worked into the red earth by thousands of walkers over hundreds of years, snaked in and out of view. In places it was so steep he was forced to grab hold of branches or stout shrubs. Now he was in . . . he consulted the map again . . . Smokum Wood. Minutes away from the caves. And minutes later he had the immense satisfaction of joining the tarmac path which led back up the valley towards the caves. It was ten to ten. The caves were not yet open but he could see, glancing down, a couple of people in the car park. He hurried away up the path. He wanted to arrive alone. To see if Stan was there. To see if the pass with his name on would really work.

'You're keen, then,' said a man at the cave entrance. The doors were not yet open, and he had emerged from a small hut, holding a torch.

'I—I've got a pass,' said Eddie, digging the piece of paper out of his pocket and nervously holding it out for inspection. He feared the man would say it wasn't a proper ticket; tell him that he would have to pay. And he didn't think, after buying the map, that he had enough money left. To be turned away now after such a great start to his adventure would be terrible. Eddie peered anxiously at the man as he examined the pass. After a quick look he just raised one eyebrow and gave Eddie a slightly quizzical glance. 'You *are* a special guest, then,' he commented, with a smile. He was around fifty, Eddie thought; spry and fit from many years of cave walking, he guessed.

'Is it OK, then?' Eddie fidgeted nervously.

'Yep. No problem,' said the guide. 'You just have to wait another few minutes for the first tour.' And he disappeared back into the hut.

Eddie sat down on a bench as the couple he had seen below reached the cave entrance. By the time the guide returned there were ten people waiting for the first tour. He opened the gate into the caves and in they went. Eddie was able to concentrate better this time while the guide, who introduced himself as Mick, went through the story of the caves, covering the discovery and the cave divers and their breakthroughs as well as the legend of the witch. He was a good talker and held the attention of his small audience well, but Eddie found himself distracted. He kept looking around for Stan. There was no sign of him. In the Witch's Kitchen he looked for the entrance to the secret passageway too, while Mick told the story of the monk defeating the witch, but could see no hint of it at all. No matter how much he shifted about and leaned from side to side, there was absolutely no evidence of any secret passageway. He was only ten minutes into the cave tour that he had been so excited about that he'd hardly slept last night—and now he was feeling deflated. And he really had to stop staring at the cave wall because Mick was shooting him uneasy looks now, obviously wondering what he was up to.

Eddie decided to relax and stop being daft. The secret passage was probably in a different part of the cave wall and he had just forgotten where. Never mind. He had another cave tour to enjoy, thanks to Stan feeling sorry for him. They moved along, leaving the Witch's Kitchen behind, tracking deeper into the cave system, along high narrow corridors and low ceilinged basin-like chambers, past the green-blue luminosity of the River Axe and on. Eddie found himself lagging behind. He couldn't stop thinking about the girl. The girl who could see in the dark. Now that was difficult to explain. Did he imagine it? Did his frightened mind just make it up while he felt his way out along the wall? After all, he had just brained himself on a stalactite. He had the bruise, just under his tufty red fringe, to prove it.

He waited on one of the short catwalks suspended high above the well-lit river until the sound of the party disappeared and he could no longer hear the guide talking above the hiss and drip of a small stream that tumbled through a nearby channel of rock. Hiss and drip. Drip and hiss. Drip. Hiss. Giggle. Hiss. Eddie jumped, startled, and looked about him. Had one of the party come back down the passage to giggle at him, dreaming alone on the catwalk? No. The giggle came again. From beneath his feet. Eddie dropped to his knees and stared through the metal gridwork platform of the walkway. He felt his eyes stretch wide, as they had in the absolute darkness of the secret cave, yesterday. Looking up at him, four or five metres below, was the girl.

Eddie gaped. She appeared to be lying flat on her back on some kind of stone shelf which protruded from the cave wall. 'How did you get down there?' he gasped. 'You'll get yourself killed!' She giggled again. Maybe she was a bit mad, thought Eddie. Maybe he should call for the guide. 'Don't move!' he called. 'I'll get help!'

'Don't be so silly, Eddie,' she called back up, smiling. 'I'm not in danger. You should come and see the roof from here. It's a much better view.'

'How—how would I do that?' He found himself whispering now, because he realized he was scared. Not of the girl, but of the guide coming back and finding them. There would be all hell let loose as soon as he saw a girl down in the cave, off the tourist path.

'If you go back now, to the place you last saw me, I will meet you there. Then I'll show you,' she said.

'But I can't! The guide will see I've gone missing. He'll get up a search party or something.'

She laughed again and it rang up above the singing of the waterfall. 'No he won't. Stan will tell him you've gone back.'

Eddie opened his mouth to ask more questions but the girl had disappeared. He stared down at where she had been, but couldn't even see the shelf of rock that she must have used to lie upon. Shivering, he stood up. He looked at the path which led on to the tour party. He could just go on now, catch them up, come out at the other end of the tour and buy an ice cream like any normal boy would. Or he could retrace his steps, alone, back through the caves, to see if a girl who appeared only to him in lonely underground chambers would be there. He gulped. He turned back.

Back across the catwalks, back through the low basin chamber with its deep river pool, back through the winding corridor with its cathedral roof, back into the Witch's Kitchen. He was breathing hard; excited and scared. The big lumpy stalagmite which was meant to be the frozen witch loomed mutely up at him beside the river. Apart from the dripping water soundtrack which was played through speakers here and there, the cavern was silent—although another tour party would surely be along soon: they went every half hour. Eddie walked towards the part that he remembered Stan shining his torch at. He got his own torch out of his backpack and shone it around hopefully. He couldn't see anything but solid rock.

Then something twinkled. Something twinkled and glowed and all of a sudden the girl was there, beckoning to him. 'Quickly,' she urged. 'People will come soon. If you're coming, come now.' She held out her pale hand and Eddie stepped forward and took it. Three seconds later they were back in the narrow slanting corridor of rock, lit by his torch and the glow she held in her left palm.

She stared across the glow at him as they moved along and beamed happily. 'Stan didn't think you'd be back this week. Not so soon. But I did. I knew you'd come back right away. I knew it.'

'Where are you taking me?' breathed Eddie. 'Slow down a bit. How come you know your way around here? Does your dad work here or something?'

They were moving fast away from the main chamber and he was feeling nervous again. He could hear the waterfall but this time it sounded as if it was off to his left and they seemed to be going downhill, along a different passage. The girl showed no sign of slowing down. She ducked her head instinctively several times, pulling him down by his arm as she did so, or he would surely have been concussed again.

'What have you got in here?' she asked, suddenly turning and tugging his backpack off his shoulder.

'Just stuff,' he shrugged.

She shrugged too and dropped it to the floor, losing interest in a second. 'How are you with heights, Eddie?' she asked.

'Um—OK. Why?' He heard a quaver in his voice and coughed it away. He didn't want her to know he was nervous.

'Can you swim?'

'Yes. I can swim. What's all this about?'

'Do you like surprises?'

'Depends on what kind.'

'This is a good kind,' said the girl, taking hold of his shoulders. 'Take a deep breath.'

Eddie did take a breath, but not an especially deep one; only a breath before another question. He never got to ask it. The girl suddenly spun him round and pointed his head towards his feet. As he gasped in surprise and shone his torch down he had one second to note the swirling water and the blackness before she pushed him over the edge.

Chapter 7

Shock robbed him of a scream. There was just no time to draw breath and shriek. He was plummeting through a curtain of water and too horrified to make a sound. The strange girl was not his friend. She was his killer.

But even as this awful realization flashed through his head, he was distracted by a sensation on his back. He was *not* falling through air and water—he was . . . *sliding*. Something smooth was at his back, slowing his rate of fall. His torch, which he was still gripping, threw flailing blooms of light in all directions, snatching at twisted plumes of water and gnarled fingers of limestone. Before he had time to guess how far he had slid, he hit the water.

Don't breathe! Don't breathe! You can't breathe yet! his freaked out brain yelled at him as he sank under, his astonished eyes still open. Then he was bobbing up again on the surface, gasping for air and flapping his arms around.

'I thought you said you could swim,' said a voice off to his right. The girl was sitting on a limestone ledge, a few feet away from him, wringing out her long hair. Now he realized that there was light in this cavern, beyond the torch he was still grimly hanging on to. It seemed to radiate more widely out of the little orb that she carried, which was set down on the rock at her feet.

'Wh-wh-what did you wanna do *that* for?' he spluttered, treading water and keeping his head up out of the whirling pool.

'You said you could swim,' she repeated. 'And that you liked surprises.'

'Well, that doesn't m-mean you can shove me down a w-waterfall without any warning!' he squawked, now striking out towards her ledge, which wasn't easy while still holding the torch, but he was determined not to lose this one. He needed it. There was no telling what might happen next. This girl was clearly insane.

He reached the ledge and she helped him up onto it, smiling. 'Sorry,' she giggled. 'But you weren't in any danger. It's just a water slide.'

Eddie sat down, shaking, on the ledge. The water

was cold, but not freezing. He dimly remembered the cave guide saying that everything was a constant temperature of eleven degrees in the caves. Cool in summer, warm in winter. Still, he couldn't stop shivering. He noticed his backpack resting, apparently only slightly damp, a few feet away.

'Here,' said the girl and put the light orb thing into his hands. It was blue and pulsing slightly and had no weight at all . . . but a kind of mass—like magnets pushing away from each other—in his cupped palms. As he stared at it, intrigued, he felt the magnetism, or whatever it was, roll out from it, up his arms, over his shoulders and head and down the rest of his body. All his hairs stood on end—he felt like a robin in winter, fluffing up to stay warm. And now he *was* warm. Dazed, he passed the orb back to the girl.

'Who *are* you?'

'I told you yesterday. My name is Gwerren.'

'Gwerren . . . right. So do you, like, *live* here? I mean . . . do your dad or your mum work here or something?'

'My grandfather works up here,' she said. 'So I come up here too.'

'And he just lets you run around in the caves by yourself?' Eddie shook his head. She couldn't be more than eleven.

'I know the caves. I'm quite safe. You'll be safe with me too. Just don't go off on your own.'

Eddie stared around at the whirlpool chamber, his racing heart slowing down. It was beautiful. The chamber was round with a low concave ceiling, much like the basin-shaped cave on the main tour—but this one still had its whirlpool, turning gently at the edges while in the middle the water coming in from above played merrily across the surface. It wasn't a huge torrent of water, which was presumably why he hadn't been dashed against a rock and killed. It was just a stream. The formation it travelled down was softened by centuries of water play to a smooth slide. He couldn't see the top of it—only two or three metres of it emerged from the ceiling, reaching down like an open scoop and dwindling to a stalactite point a few feet short of the water below.

He swallowed and breathed deeply, trying to calm himself further. Gwerren's blue light thing had dried him off as well as warmed him through, he noticed, but he was still majorly spooked.

'So—how do we get back up?' he asked, eyeing the waterslide. He did not fancy trying to climb it.

'Not up *there*, silly!' Her chuckle rang out above the endless hissing and bubbling of the water. 'Come on, follow me. You need some cheese.'

Eddie got to his feet, shaking his head. This was getting more surreal by the minute. 'Cheese,' he murmured, picking up the torch and his backpack and following her. 'Of course.'

She led him along another passage which opened up behind her as they stood. She put the blue glowing thing on her shoulder and it lit the way. He couldn't see any electricity cables, though, or any lamps attached to the walls or ceiling. Gwerren walked confidently ahead, inclining her head or swinging her hips to one side as the narrow passage demanded. It was so smooth and instinctive she was like water herself. She was wearing shorts and a T-shirt again and, he noticed with surprise, no shoes at all.

'Don't you stub your toe all the time, with no shoes on?' he asked. He was *always* stubbing a toe, himself.

She laughed again. 'No! My toes know this place. Here—up we go!' And now she turned left into an even narrower passage which led steeply upwards. She sped up it with ease and then turned to offer him a hand as he struggled along behind her.

'No—I'm good,' he puffed. He was beginning to feel lumpy and clumsy and it made him embarrassed. She shrugged and went on. A few more twists and turns and they were in a small room, not much bigger than his bedroom at home. It smelled of old socks. Gwerren flicked a switch and normal yellow electric lights clicked on. There were wooden shelves at every angle of the walls with big round waxy shapes on them. Eddie grinned and started to laugh. 'Will you get into trouble?' he checked as she knelt down and pulled a drawer out of the base of one of the shelf units. In it were packages wrapped up in waxed paper. She selected a small one.

'They don't mind. They don't notice, anyway. This is the nicest lot—not too old.' She handed him a small yellow wedge of genuine Cheddar cheese. Eddie knew it was matured here—he'd seen some stacked up in a passage during the tour yesterday. You could buy it in the gift shop.

He was still far too overwhelmed to be hungry, but he nibbled on the edge of the cheese anyway, and then found himself hooked by its wonderful tangy flavour. A minute later he'd wolfed it all down.

'Good, isn't it?' grinned Gwerren, taking a bite from her own slice. 'Stan says it's cave fruit!' She giggled again and Eddie decided that maybe she wasn't insane. Her laugh was nice. He had to admit that.

'Is Stan your grandfather?' he asked. She nodded.

'Why did he give me the pass? Why did he want me to come back?'

She tilted her head to one side and regarded him with her large silver-lilac eyes. 'He thought you might . . . belong.'

Eddie felt uneasy. He wasn't at all sure about what she meant. Her words made him think of people who were caught up in sinister cults.

'Belong? Belong with who—I mean, whom? I mean . . . what might I belong to?'

Gwerren's face was suddenly vague and distant and her eyelids fluttered. She raised her palms to the ceiling and breathed: 'To the caves . . . to the caves . . . the caaaaaaaves . . . They want you, Eddie! Can't you feel it? The caaaaaaaaves want you for e-e-e-ever!'

Eddie stepped back, wishing he'd laid off the cheese.

She let out a hoot of laughter. 'Oh, Ed! I really had you going!' She hooted some more and then sniffed and sighed happily. 'You *are* easy! No—the caves don't care either way. Stan just thought you might like to play. He knew I was a bit bored on my own. That's all.'

Eddie let out a shaky laugh. 'Riii-ight.' He wiped his brow. He felt pretty warm. Must be all the fermenting dairy produce around him.

'Do you?' asked Gwerren.

'What?'

65

'Want to play?'

'What—here?'

'Well . . . yes. There's a lot to show you. Unless you'd rather be back with your cousins, of course.' She shrugged and looked at her feet but she was biting her lip and trying not to smile.

'You saw my cousins, then,' he grinned.

'The singing, dancing ones? Yes. I thought they might bring down a few stalactites with their high notes. And then your lovely older cousin who only likes excitement through a little glass screen.'

'Yep—that's Damon. And no—no I *don't* want to go back to them. Not until I have to.'

'Good. So let's play.'

Eddie checked his watch. It was 1.15 p.m. He hesitated. 'Well . . . I can stay a bit longer. But I have to go at about two.' He had told Auntie Kath he'd be back in the afternoon and walking back would take nearly an hour. Get back much later than three and he might get into trouble. More importantly, he had promised Uncle Wilf that he'd go in and read to him after lunch.

'All right,' said Gwerren, 'something quick, before you go. Come on!' She seized his hand and ran quickly back down the cheese-store steps and into the winding rock corridor. In a now familiar routine, Eddie ran along

66

behind her, watching her movements and then mimicking them to avoid getting a limestone smack in the head or elbow or hip. His fear had left him and only excitement now bubbled through his veins as she sped ahead, the blue glow in her hand throwing wild shadows in all directions. He didn't bother to switch on his torch now. His eyes had grown accustomed to Gwerren's light.

After three or four minutes of cave-dashing which took them up and down and off to the left, they rounded a corner into another large cave. He stood still and gazed around him, fascinated. This cave had no stalactites or stalagmites at all, and no water running through. It was round and curved away smoothly in all directions. A hole in the cupped ceiling led off up into blackness like a chimney. Nothing appeared to drip from it. But it was the floor that was most interesting. About a metre from Eddie's feet it fell away in a steep, swooping slope. The whole cave floor was a wide, deep bowl. The limestone here was so smooth it glistened and Eddie crouched down to run his fingers along it, half expecting it to be wet, even though his other senses informed him that they were in a dry place. The other senses were right. The rock was dry—just incredibly smooth. He stood again, feeling as though he was on the edge of a vast empty soup tureen.

'Wow,' said Eddie, looking around at Gwerren

who was still at the entrance behind him. She beamed, set her blue light down on the floor again, and then turned back into the passage and picked up something from behind a rocky outcrop.

'Here you go!' and she threw a piece of material at him. It was a large, quite finely woven sack. She had one too.

Eddie stared at it and then back at his new friend. 'Well?' she said. 'What are you waiting for?' And then she stepped past him, threw the sacking down, leaped onto it and slid over the rim of the cave bowl in one fluid movement. She gave a whoop as she sped down the curve, across the middle of the bowl and up the other side. As she reached the opposite rim she twisted in the air, like a skateboarder, and flipped back round to repeat the journey. Eddie lost no time in joining her. He set down his sacking, sat on it, holding the edges up at his hips, and then cannoned off the edge.

It was exhilarating! Like a fairground ride. He whooped too. It couldn't be helped. The velocity for the first few steep metres was fantastic and shooting across the middle and up the other side was easy. Flipping around for the return journey was a little harder. He stalled and ended up slithering down backwards to the middle. He had to stand up and gather up the sack and climb back out again. He was soon sliding again, copying Gwerren as she spun and turned and slid on her sack at top speed.

'What *is* this place?' he shouted as they shot past each other. 'It's brilliant. How come the tour guides don't bring people here? They'd go nuts for this! Whoo-hoo! Watch me! I'm twisting back now!'

'It used to be a whirlpool, thousands of years ago,' called back Gwerren. 'Like the one with the water slide. Some big rocks would have been caught up in here and then just gone round and round and round, scouring out this chamber, until they shrank away themselves and got washed on down the water way. But the water ran lower in the ground and hasn't been here for centuries. That's why it's all dry now. Good, isn't it?'

'It's fantastic!' sang Eddie. He cannoned into Gwerren more than once and she squeaked and shoved him back down the slope as he tried to climb up, laughing. He could have gone on sliding and whizzing up and down and tumbling off and clambering back and starting all over again for hours. In the end it was Gwerren who slid and spun herself expertly up to the cave entrance and skipped up on to her feet, pulling the sack up behind her.

'Come on,' she said, picking up the blue light orb. 'You have to go now.'

Eddie slid to a stop at the bottom of the bowl and stared at his watch. It was past two o'clock. He sighed.

'Come again another day,' said Gwerren.

'OK—how about Thursday? Say, about eleven o'clock? I'll meet you in—'

'I'll know when you're here. And where,' said Gwerren, helping him up out of the bowl. 'Just come whenever. I'll find you.'

'Yeah but—'

'Don't go off the tour path though,' she added. 'You don't know your way around and it can be dangerous. Always wait for me in the electric areas. Where the yellow lights are.'

'OK—by the secret passage that Stan showed me. I know exactly where that is.'

She smiled and turned to lead the way back.

'No you don't,' she said. 'You won't ever find it without me or Stan, so don't try to.'

Eddie thought she was a little bit cocky, really, but he let it go. He had had a brilliant, brilliant day. 'Hang on though—have we got to climb back up the water slide?' He checked, suddenly anxious again. 'I haven't got to get soaked again, have I?'

'No,' she laughed. 'I'll take you back the dry way.'

She led him up and up, along winding cave passages that he could never hope to connect up into any kind of map in his mind. None of them had electricity cables or lights, but the blue light she carried was good enough to travel by.

'What is that in your hand?' he asked. 'Is it one of those phosphorus light-stick things—you know, like you get in camping shops?'

'A bit like that,' she agreed. 'Here you go.' And suddenly she reached out her hand towards what looked like a blank wall of rock and pulled a metal ring embedded in it. And the rock was *not* rock. It was a door. An ancient wooden door which had aged to the same colour as the rock around them. As it creaked open a shaft of the most brilliant light blasted into the dark, making him blink, dazzled. Gwerren disappeared behind the door and as he stepped out he heard her say, 'See you again one day, Eddie,' and then the door closed and he was in the wooded valley above the caves.

He spun around to see the door—it must be something the guides used in emergencies, perhaps. But to his astonishment, there was no door there. Just another of the familiar rocky outcrops that characterized the Mendip hills. There was a flat smooth plane on this one, which looked a bit *like* a door in shape—but it was not a door. Frowning, he stepped up to it and ran his hands all over it, feeling for cracks or buttons or some secret spring that might open it. But he knew this was rock. Only rock. There was no door. He stepped back, dazed.

'So how did I get here?' he asked himself, aloud. He sat down on the slope, gazing around the valley. There was not a soul here. Everyone else had gone in and out of the caves by the usual route, from the car park in the village to the walkway to the entrance and then back out through the dinosaur valley play area, the mill museum, the amusement arcade, and the gift shop.

What had just happened to him? He had been pushed down a hole and nearly drowned in an underground plunge-pool and then dried out by a weird blue light given to him by a strange pale girl, then fed cheese, and given a slide-ride in an ancient bowl of rock.

Eddie made up his mind never to say that out loud to anyone.

Chapter 8

He didn't get back until well after three, but nobody seemed to have noticed he was a bit late. The twins were biting the glitter nail varnish off their nails while watching Disney Channel and Damon was up on the computer in his room, playing an on-line game, hammering the keyboard angrily and shouting out words that would never have got out past the Net Nanny if he'd typed them.

Eddie stashed his backpack in the under-stairs cupboard and wandered into the kitchen. He had noticed an unfamiliar car parked outside the house and expected to see his aunt chatting with one of her friends over a cup of tea, but there was nobody there. He could hear voices though, in Uncle Wilf's room. He walked to the door and pushed it open a little. Through the gap he could see a woman in a navy cardigan sitting on the end of Uncle Wilf's bed, a cup of tea in her hand. He heard his aunt, out of view, speaking.

'Yes, I think he does get a bit lonely when we're all out,' she was saying, in a rather treacly voice. 'Don't you, Uncle?'

Uncle Wilf muttered something which Eddie couldn't make out. He felt a prickle go up the back of his neck, but he didn't know why. Warm air pulsed around the edge of the door. That was odd. Normally only cold, rather damp air came from Uncle Wilf's room. Auntie Kath must have put the heater on for longer today.

'Of course, we'd love to spend more time with Uncle but the children have a very busy life just keeping up with school and clubs and dancing,' went on Auntie Kath. 'My daughters are championship level disco dancers, did I mention?'

'You did,' smiled the lady in the blue cardigan. She turned her attention to Uncle Wilf, who was out of sight of Eddie, obviously in his armchair at the foot of the bed. 'Now, Uncle Wilf,' she began.

'I'm sorry—have we met before?' said Uncle Wilf in an ironic tone.

'He gets a bit confused,' said Auntie Kath, quickly.

'Are you related to me?' continued Uncle Wilf, to the lady in the blue cardigan. 'Only I didn't realize I had another niece.'

She smiled again. 'No—I'm not, of course. It was just a—a figure of speech. May I call you Wilf?'

'You may call me Mr Harrison,' he replied. Eddie grinned. Good for him!

'Mr Harrison—I am here to have a little chat with you about how you're managing here with Kath and the family.' She paused but Uncle Wilf did not reply, so she went on. 'Kath tells me you're not very mobile these days; that you need help to get about—to have a bath and so on.'

'I can manage fine,' said Uncle Wilf. His voice was flat and guarded.

'But you do need help—if you need to have a bath or . . . or . . . '

'I can manage,' he repeated. 'I can get to the toilet, if that's what you mean. I don't need to be wheeled in there yet. And I have a shower. If you can call it that.'

Auntie Kath sighed, and through the other crack of the door jamb Eddie saw her shaking her head and smiling sadly. 'You can manage . . . sometimes, Uncle. Most of the time. Yes—most of the time, I would say. Really, you do *very well* for a man of your years and I know you've got your pride and would hate to be a burden.' She walked across the room now, to the top end of the bed, coming into view again at the wider crack of the slightly open door. Eddie saw her flip back the duvet and smile and sigh again. She pointed to the sheet, halfway down the bed, and looked meaningfully at the visitor. Even from his awkward viewpoint he could make out the large damp patch on the sheet.

There was a long silence and then Eddie heard a rustle of paper and saw that the visitor had a clip-board on her lap.

'Kathy tells me you get a bit forgetful at times, Wil—er . . . Mr Harrison,' she said.

'Doesn't everyone?' he countered.

'Of course! I know *I* do.' A pen was clicked. 'But just so that I have some idea of where you are on the forgetfulness scale, can you just do a little quiz with me?'

'Who are you? Dale Winton?'

Eddie laughed silently to himself, but then stopped short when he heard no laughter in the room beyond. Instead Auntie Kath said, carefully, 'No, Uncle. This is Jackie Biggs. You remember? I told you she was coming!'

'You did not!'

A sigh. 'Yes, I did, Uncle. You just forgot. She's *not* Dale Winton. *Or* Carol Vorderman.' She whispered to Jackie Biggs now. 'He thought *I* was Carol Vorderman last week, bless him! Kept asking for a P.

Or maybe he actually wanted a *pee* . . . who knows, these days?'

Eddie stepped back and stood up straight, feeling a chill run through him. He had a really horrible idea that something most unpleasant was happening. Uncle Wilf had *never* mistaken Auntie Kath for anyone else. He was *not* losing his marbles! Eddie moved close to the door again.

'Anyway, back to our quiz, Mr Harrison,' simpered Jackie Biggs. 'Can you tell me what year this is?' Uncle Wilf chuckled but did not reply. 'Who is the Prime Minister?' pressed his quizmistress. No reply. 'How about money? What does a pint of milk cost? 49p, £4.90, or £40?' A long, leaden silence.

Eventually Auntie Kath said, 'The lady's only trying to help, Uncle. We're all trying to help. We only want what's best for you, you know.'

'Is that so?' said Uncle Wilf. 'Then get this smug cow out of my room. I want to watch telly.'

Auntie Kath protested in shocked tones but Jackie Biggs shushed her. 'It's all right. They often get this way,' she said, as she got to her feet and gathered up her clipboard and bag. 'It's understandable. Let's leave your uncle in peace and go and have a chat in the garden.'

Eddie shot across the kitchen and into the hallway

77

just in time. As his aunt and the visitor came out of Uncle Wilf's room he walked back in, casually. 'Hi, Auntie Kath,' he called. 'Oh—hello!' as he pretended to see the visitor for the first time.

'Hello, Eddie,' said his aunt. 'Did you have a nice bird watching trip?'

'Yeah, it was great, thanks.' He eyed the woman next to her, questioningly.

Auntie Kath turned to her. 'This is my nephew, who I also have to look after this summer, because my sister-in-law is ill. It's my Christian duty, obviously, but I don't know how I manage it all, really.' There was a wobble in her voice. 'I just don't know . . . '

The woman smiled at his aunt and patted her shoulder. 'You're doing an amazing job, Kath. Amazing. But everyone has their limit, eh? Don't be too hard on yourself.' And they both went off out into the garden, leaving Eddie standing still in the kitchen, feeling slightly sick. He didn't know what this was about, but he had such a bad feeling.

Uncle Wilf was staring at the TV when he went in, but even though the picture was actually not too bad today, Eddie could tell he wasn't seeing it at all.

'What's all that about, then?' he said, sitting down on the end of the bed, avoiding the wet patch.

'Don't get old, Eddie,' said Uncle Wilf.

'O-K,' said Eddie. 'But that would mean dying young.'

'No, don't do that either. Just don't—don't be an old fool like me.'

'What do you mean?'

The old man sighed and ran a hand through his thin grey hair. 'Nothing. There's no point bellyaching about it now. What's done is done. Probably for the best anyway.'

'What are you talking about?' Eddie's growing alarm made his voice shrill. 'Uncle Wilf—what was that woman asking you questions for? Why was Auntie Kath showing her your wet bed.'

'My wet bed,' muttered Uncle Wilf. 'Not *my* wet bed!'

Eddie fidgeted, uncomfortable. 'Well . . . it *is* a pretty big wet patch. You have to admit. Didn't you notice it, when you got up? I mean . . . it happens to everyone once in a while, doesn't it.'

'Sniff it,' said Uncle Wilf.

'You what?'

'You heard me. Sniff it.'

'Uncle Wilf . . . '

'Scared of a bit of urine, are you? Thought you were made of tougher stuff than that. You go and sniff it and tell me what you think.'

Eddie got up and edged up the bed. He pulled up the duvet and, grimacing, lowered his nose to the tell-tale yellowy stain. Then he stopped. He did indeed know what a wet bed smelt like. It wasn't something he was going to broadcast, but he had been a bed wetter himself, until he was seven. He knew how it felt to wake up from a dream of having a wee only to find, to your horror, that you were going in your bed. He knew the unhappy task of stripping off his bedclothes and ramming them in the laundry basket in the early hours, and creeping back to the dry end of the mattress with a spare blanket, chilly and ashamed, in spite of his parents' reassurances that it happened to everyone sometimes. And he certainly knew exactly what it smelt like.

Not like this. Eddie sniffed again—harder. He stood up and stared across at Uncle Wilf, puzzled. He prodded the wet patch and then put the tip of his finger on his tongue. He was right. 'Apple juice,' he said.

'Yep,' said Uncle Wilf.

'So . . . did you spill it or something?'

'Nope,' said Uncle Wilf.

Eddie sat down next to him again, his mind winding around a very nasty thought. Uncle Wilf had only a beaker of water next to his bed, on the little

80

table that also held the lamp. And if he had spilt anything, why would it be right down inside the bed and not at the top, where he was drinking it?

'So . . . you think someone else spilt it there.'

Uncle Wilf nodded and let his eyes wander back to the TV.

'Deliberately.'

He nodded again.

'Why?'

The man shifted around in his seat to stare at the boy. 'Come on, now. Use your brain. Who do you think that woman was? Social Services, of course. Your aunt's had enough of me. She's shipping me out.'

'What? Where to?'

'To Incontinence Acres Rest Home For Dribblers, of course! The only council run home left in the district. Hope they take me on a Friday. That's Spam fritters and bingo day.'

Eddie was too appalled to laugh. 'But . . . she can't! I mean—how can she? You're her uncle. You— you paid all that money so she could look after you and . . . and—'

'Nothing was on paper, Eddie,' sighed Uncle Wilf. 'Nothing was signed. Nothing legal. It was all very friendly. Very sensible. I was going to go into sheltered flats, you see. That made sense—a place of your own and someone to pop in and check on you. That's what I had planned. But Kath and John said, why don't you have an annexe on our place, eh? A nice little flat of your own and then *we* can be the ones looking in on you. You'll get some home cooking too.'

'Annexe? So what happened to the annexe?' Eddie demanded.

'This is it.'

'What—a grotty old garage and a rubbish toilet and shower and no proper heating or TV and—and—*home cooking*?' Somehow this last promise made him more angry than anything else. Nobody in their right mind would describe Auntie Kath's frozen convenience meals as home cooking. They were just like her character when it came to Eddie and Uncle Wilf— quite nice looking on the cardboard. Nothing much inside.

'That's not fair! That's so—*so*—not fair! We have to do something! We have to . . . we have to . . . '

Uncle Wilf took Eddie's hand in his own gnarled one. 'Take it easy. Take it easy. I shouldn't have told you all that stuff. It's nothing for you to worry about.'

'It *is* something for me to worry about!' protested Eddie, his voice thick with tears. 'Of course it is!'

'It's probably for the best. Like I said. I mean, it's not as if it's a five star hotel here, now is it?'

'But—but what if they make you do bingo and stuff?'

Uncle Wilf laughed then—really laughed. He wiped his eyes and grinned at Eddie as the chuckles subsided. 'If I get a nice warm bath two or three times a week, it'll be worth any amount of bingo. You never know, I might even like it. And the women'll be all over me. Four to one, it is, in those places. All those women, hardly any men! I'll be a babe magnet. I'll be fighting them off with my rolled up Saga magazine.'

Eddie sniffed and laughed a bit.

'Look—I know how it goes,' said Uncle Wilf. 'They'll be back to tell me about this lovely little place they've found. They'll ask me to go on a nice trip to have a look at it. Want to come with me, when they do? Eh? You can run around and chat up the old ladies—find out which ones have still got their own teeth, eh? I'm not snogging any denture queens.'

Eddie grinned. 'Yeah. Of course I'll come—if Auntie Kath will let me.'

'I'll tell her I won't go unless you come too. Now. Enough of all this. Let's do the conundrum.' And they turned back to *Countdown* and tried to pretend everything was fine.

Chapter 9

'What's this?' Gwerren took the bar from his hand and stared at it.

'It's a Star Bar. What did you think it was?' He shrugged. 'I got us one each. Good for energy, yeah? If we're really going to hike down to that lower cave you were on about.'

She nodded slowly, still staring at the Star Bar and turning it over in her palm. The plastic wrapping crackled slightly. She murmured, 'Cadbury's.' She pronounced it *cad-berries*.

'Blimey, haven't you ever seen a bar of chocolate before?' Eddie snorted.

'Of course I have. I've eaten cad-berries before. It's lovely. Thank you.'

'Oh—I get it. You're from one of those funny families that only eats organic raw veg and stuff. Wholefood freaks. Is that what you're like?'

She shook her head and gave him a rather blank look. 'We eat all kinds of things,' she said. 'We eat cad-berries sometimes. Just not very often, that's all. You don't have to call us freaks.'

'Sorry,' said Eddie, grinning. 'Just having you on. You're always winding *me* up, aren't you? I still haven't forgotten *the ca-a-a-aves neee-eee-eeed me* . . . '

Gwerren smiled and tucked the chocolate into a pocket of the loose top she was wearing over her shorts. She did *look* a bit 'new age', Eddie thought. There were no labels or even zips on her clothes—they all looked hand-made. And she still had nothing on her feet.

'Come on then,' said Gwerren. 'I'll take you to the warm cave—if you've got time. It will take us a while to get there. How much time have you got?'

Eddie checked his watch—Gwerren didn't wear one. It was 11.15. He had said he'd be back for tea, which was around five. There was no rush. 'Ages,' he said. 'Four hours. It won't take us *that* long.'

'Time moves strangely here,' she said, echoing what Stan had said to him, the first day they'd met.

Stan had met him twice, since, at the gate to the caves. He had taken responsibility for the boy with the season ticket, waving him past the tour guides, who now said hello to him and went on their way

85

with their tour schedules, never asking him what he was doing. Clearly Stan had explained to them that Eddie was with him. Like a work experience kid or something. Then Stan would take him some way into the caves and just leave him to wait for Gwerren— who would mysteriously arrive within a few minutes. Today was his third visit to Gwerren and he was beginning to feel as if the caves were his back garden. He always brought along his backpack with supplies, including a spare torch and batteries (he had used up all his holiday money now, buying these from the shop on the corner) and a sandwich and some drink. He was an explorer and he was kitted out for it. He just wished he could afford one of those helmets with lights on, so he could have both hands free while he was clambering along after his new friend.

'Come on then,' said Gwerren. She led him off along a passage they'd been through before and then sharply down to the right through a gap which he had not seen last time. This had happened several times now. He was regularly astonished by it. How was it that he hadn't seen these passages leading off before? Gwerren said he just 'didn't know how to look'.

'So, where does your family live, then?' he puffed, trying to keep up with her. She moved like a lizard, sometimes, scampering fast and sure across the slanting rock, her long fingers and toes anchoring her securely at all angles.

'Quite near here,' she said.

'What—in the village?' There was a small but thriving village beneath the caves, which had grown up centuries ago around the paper mill that used to run on the power of the River Axe.

'It is a kind of village,' she said. 'Mind your head.'

He ducked just in time as the ceiling of the cave passage suddenly swooped down low. Very low. Seconds later they were crawling along on their bellies, even more like lizards, and his backpack was in his hand, being tugged along beside him. The rock below his palms and knees sloped steeply down and the rock above was skimming the tufty hair on his crown. If he'd left the pack on his back he might very well have got stuck.

'Are you sure this is safe?' he asked, squeaking slightly. Although he had grown to feel increasingly at home in the caves with Gwerren, he had never quite lost a thrill of anxiety that the whole limestone playground could suddenly fall on his head.

'Just wriggle and slide—like an eel,' she called back. 'You'll fit. Maybe not five years from now, but today you'll fit.'

He controlled the anxiety trying to get a grip on

him and kept his breathing steady. He stayed calm, even when the gap in the rock became so shallow that he had to turn his head sideways and slide his cheek along the limestone bed to get through and keep up with Gwerren.

A minute later, though, the cave widened out again and the headroom shot up dramatically. He was able to stand up and stretch out his arms and put his pack back on over his shoulders. Gwerren paused and looked back at him. 'Are you all right?' she asked.

'Yes. Thought I was going to lose my ear back there, though! Are we nearly there?'

'About halfway. Check your watch.'

Eddie did so. He was astonished to see that nearly an hour had passed. It hadn't felt like more than fifteen minutes, scrambling through the rock. Gwerren noticed his surprise. 'Time moves . . . ' she began.

' . . . strangely here,' finished Eddie. 'You're not wrong. We'd better speed up or we won't make it there and back.'

'No—rest. Let's eat some cad-berries,' advised Gwerren, sitting down cross-legged on the stone floor of the cave passage. In the light from his torch and her blue glowing thing, which was sitting on her shoulder again today, like a living creature, he could see more of the curtain-style limestone formations rippling down from the narrow ceiling above them and the tell-tale shallow ridges curving across the floor, sculpted by an ancient river, long since gone.

He took out his Star Bar and watched Gwerren take out hers. He expected it to be flattened by the tight squeeze through the rock passage, but although his was a bit squashed, Gwerren's looked perfect. She tore delicately into the wrapper and peeled it carefully away at the top, revealing the smooth chocolate log. She stared at it for a moment, and then bit into it. Her eyes widened as she encountered soft toffee and sweet peanut. She clearly hadn't had a Star Bar before.

'Good?' he asked, grinning and munching his own. Star Bars were his favourite.

'Mmmm!' she enthused, but she only took one more bite. She closed her eyes as she ate it and looked as if it was an intense experience.

'So . . . how often do you eat chocolate then?' he asked. She was an odd girl, and there was no getting away from it.

'Just . . . sometimes,' she murmured, tucking the wrapping tightly back round the remaining bar. 'You couldn't have this every day, could you?' She sounded slightly breathy.

'You could if you were Damon,' he said. 'About four times a day, in fact.'

'No!' she breathed, getting to her feet. Her large eyes looked even larger and she bit her lip and giggled.

'Wait a minute!' Eddie got to his feet too. 'You hardly *ever* have this stuff, do you? Look at you! You're getting all twitchy and sugar-rushy!'

'I don't know what you mean.' She giggled and then darted away down the passage at top speed. 'Come on! Come on! We haven't got all day!' She moved even more like a lizard now—a gecko—swift and slightly mad, leaping from left to right and running a little way up the low sloping walls, as if she had to get rid of a sudden flood of energy.

Eddie laughed loudly as he ran after her, the sound echoing back fast off the rock walls. 'You're having a sugar rush! Look at you! You'd better not have any more of that before tomorrow or you'll be running across the ceiling!'

It was a race now just to keep up with her and more than once he had to shout, 'Wait! Gwerren! Wait!' Which was probably why it was only another ten minutes of steep descent before they reached what she called the 'Warm Cave'. They finally stopped in a tall sleeve of rock, reaching up and up into jagged points which folded out of sight. Along the tear-shaped base of the cave was a lake. Or a slow moving river, most likely. Gwerren set her blue light down on a rocky ledge and tapped it. It grew much, much brighter, filling the cave with brightness and sharp dramatic shadows. Eddie turned his torch into a lantern, as he had with the torch he'd lost on the day he'd first met her, and cast a little gold light among the blue. The softly lit water meandered past them, blue and gold and glowing, but what was more remarkable was the steam coming off it. Eddie stared. *Was* it steam? How could it be? Nothing got above eleven degrees in the caves, did it? That's what the guides said. Steady temperature—unchanging at any time of the year; it was why the cheese matured there so well.

'How . . . what . . . I mean—what is this?' he murmured.

'The warm cave,' said Gwerren. 'There are more like this. You just have to go deeper to find them.'

'Are you telling me that this water is . . . is *warm*?'

'Can't you feel it?' she laughed. 'Come on! Come in!' And, pausing only to put the remains of her Star Bar by the blue light, she ran straight into the water with a dainty series of splashes. She turned in it, hidden from the chin downwards in its ripples, just her fingers breaking the surface. 'It's not dangerous. You can stand up in most of it. It gets deeper towards the back of the cave, but you can't be pulled under and on down, because you can't fit through the gap in the rocks. Come in!'

Eddie stared at her in amazement. Never in anything he'd ever read about the caves in the Mendips (and he'd read a lot in the last week) had there been any mention of hot underground springs. Of course, he knew they existed in the UK. They had natural warm spas at Bath—and the city of Southampton heated its civic centre with hot underground springs. But he didn't know about such a phenomenon here. He put down his backpack and took off his sweatshirt. He took off his trainers and socks and then pondered over his jeans. Could he deal with Gwerren seeing him in his underpants? He didn't think denim would be a good thing to wear in water. At this point Gwerren ducked right under the water, her bare toes flipping up into view. He used the distraction to shuffle off his jeans. His pants looked like swimming trunks, pretty much, anyway. He took an excited breath and then ran for the water, his bare toes registering the warmth even in the limestone. The pool, curling around his ankles, knees, then hips, then chest, was like a bath. It had a pungent earthy smell—a good *cave-y* smell. He squeaked, in spite of himself, with delight, splashing his arms down into it. Gwerren's head popped back up through the water.

'It's good, isn't it?' she beamed. 'It's warm! It's always exactly this warm!'

Beneath his feet the underwater bedrock of the cave was smooth and curved away down, rather like the slope of a swimming pool, made for the job. He shuffled along until it fell away far enough to make him edge back again. Gwerren began to swim away from him, towards the far corner of the pool, following the steady current. He kicked away and followed her. As he swam, the warm water rippling past his chin, he realized that the current was getting stronger. Gwerren was at the corner of the pool now, hanging on to an outcrop above her and grinning across at him.

'Don't worry,' she said. 'It pulls you along hard here because it's going off down a funnel—to the lower springs. But it can't pull you through. You're too big.'

He barely needed to kick at all now—he was gliding fast towards her, propelled by the unseen force beneath him. With a shout he caught the same ridge of rock as she had, in time to stop himself being whacked into the limestone wall below it.

'Now you have to try to get back!' she said. 'It's quite hard to swim back. Wait a minute before you try.' Eddie waited, beaming at her, thrilled with this

93

latest discovery. Imagine what people would say if they knew!

Now Gwerren took a deep breath and pushed hard against the rock wall and back out across the pool. She was very fit—that much Eddie had worked out—but she still made little grunts of effort as she struck out and made her slow way back, cutting a temporary channel through the water. When he followed her, Eddie wondered for a few seconds if he could make it; the pull of the outflowing current behind and below him was like tough elastic attached to his hips and shoulders, but he was determined not to show himself up and so, with even louder grunting, he pushed hard away from the rock wall and did a steady, determined front crawl. He got himself back across almost as fast as Gwerren had, and as he relaxed, half floating, half sitting in the shallows, out of reach of the current, Gwerren got out. She shook herself, like a dog, and the water fanned out of her light clothes. She pulled back her long pale hair and twisted it into a knot, raining a shower of drops onto the cave floor. Her limbs were slim and athletic and her hands and feet seemed always to be rippling with movement and energy. Not for the first time, Eddie found himself wondering *what* she was, as much as who she was. He had never met anyone like her. He could not picture her in a house or a shop. He could not imagine her watching Disney Channel or performing 'Boogie Wonderland'; couldn't see her giggling and whispering to schoolfriends in the corner of the playground and looking at magazines like *Gem* and *Sugar* and discussing who was the most gorgeous in the latest boy band or TV soap. In short, she was unlike every other girl he knew. She hadn't even made a funny comment about him swimming in just his pants; hadn't even appeared to notice.

But now she was looking at his pile of clothes and picking something up—his watch. 'Oops,' she said. 'You'd better get dried off and dressed. We've got to head back—and it's all uphill.'

She was right. It was nearly three. Where had the time gone? They had a long climb back out of the caves and then he'd have to walk back over the hill. He got out of the water fast and she came over to him with the blue light and a few seconds later he was more or less dry.

'How do you *do* that?' he asked.

'Come on, get your clothes on,' she said. 'Hurry up. I don't want to get you into trouble.'

The climb back was a lot harder, of course, and soon he had lost that wonderfully clean, softened feeling the warm mineral-laden water had lent his skin, and was sweating as he climbed hard, trying to keep up with Gwerren. After twenty minutes of climbing and walking and sometimes belly-wriggling up and along and around the unforgiving tunnels, Gwerren, running along a high-ceilinged passage, suddenly stopped dead and put her hands out behind her to stop him too.

'Wait!' she whispered. 'Switch off your torch. Be quiet. And still. Don't move.'

He instantly obeyed. He had never heard this tone in her voice before. It was a tone you did not argue with. He peered over her shoulder, trying to work out what had caused it, but her blue glow had dimmed to almost nothing and blackness surged in around them. For more than a minute he saw nothing and heard nothing other than the occasional drip of water off to his left. Then he felt Gwerren tense and tensed himself. There were voices! Voices this far down! They were still nowhere near the tourist trail with its electric lights and guide rails. Who could it be?

Gwerren turned to him, touched his shoulder, and whispered, 'Cave divers.'

And a few seconds later there were random beams of jerky torchlight, and then they stepped into view in the opening to the next part of the passageway. They were kitted up in cave diving gear—wet suits, canisters on their backs, hardhats with lights attached, goggles hanging at their necks. Three men, muddy and tired from the day's exploration. The last in the line stopped. 'Whoa, John! Chris!' he called and Eddie started, shocked. They were going to meet! What would fully grown cave divers make of a couple of kids running around down here? The last of the men paused by the opening where he and Gwerren stood, motion-less, barely breathing in the dark. The light from the man's helmet swept across them in a swift arc, throwing his face, behind, into shadow. Eddie swallowed hard. He didn't know what to say to the man.

'What is it, Dan?' called another man.

'Not sure,' said Dan. His light continued to arc back and forth in their faces. Eddie was confused. Could the man not *see* them? His cave-diving mates now joined him, adding their own beams to the dance of light across Eddie's face. Gwerren stood in front of him, still as the rock around them. They must surely be looking right at her—so why were they not exclaiming in amazement? Or perhaps in recognition, if she was known to them through Stan?

'Looked a bit like a gap there, for a second. A crack, maybe. What do you reckon, John?' murmured Dan, still looking directly at them but clearly seeing only a wall of rock. Now the man next to him—John, presumably—stepped closer and ran his fingers along the surface of a cave wall which absolutely WAS NOT THERE, as far as Eddie could see . . . and yet . . . and yet . . . for the man on the other side, it *was* as solid rock. Solid, dense rock. Eddie could even make out the flattening of the man's dirty fingers as they pressed against the invisible wall between them.

'Come on,' said the other man; the youngest of the three, who must be Chris. His fair hair gleamed in the light of their reflected torch beams. 'There's a steak pie at the Hunter's Inn with my name on it!'

'OK,' said Dan, and he and his fellow cavers moved on. They were out of sight in seconds, the beams of their torches throwing back for less than a minute, their voices audible to Eddie for another four or five minutes. In all that time Gwerren did not move. She remained as frozen as the fabled Witch of Wookey, until Eddie tapped her shoulder.

'What was that?' he whispered. 'What *was* that? They looked right at us. They didn't *see* us.'

Gwerren's solid shoulder relaxed back into flesh again. 'They just don't know how to look.'

'Oh, come *on*! They didn't just look! They touched! Didn't you see that? That guy pressed his fingers on—on a cave wall which they thought they could see—and he felt it too! There was like a—a force field—right there between us!' Eddie switched his torch

98

back on and there was the entrance to the passageway which the cavers had peered through—only they had not seen it. He walked towards it, expecting to bash into the force field. But nothing stopped his passing. Nothing even slowed him down or made the gentlest of protests against his movement. No odd breezes or magnetic pulses or anything—anything at all—to suggest that there had ever been anything but thin air between him and Gwerren and the cavers.

Eddie turned to look at Gwerren. Her blue light was back on her shoulder again. She was smiling and looking away beyond him. 'Time for you to get back,' she said, pushing past him on into the passage, past the point of the force field that Eddie could not find.

He felt freaked. Freaked and a bit angry.

'Stop acting like I'm an idiot!' he shouted after her as she bounded swiftly ahead. 'Tell me what you know!'

But she didn't. She wouldn't answer him at all. Not anything.

'Stop being such a drama queen! Just tell me what's going on!' he called, sounding snappy and narky. She just kept moving away from him—never far enough away that he lost her and couldn't follow, but always too far away to have to answer him. *Now* she was acting like an ordinary girl, he thought. She was sulking.

She took him to the side door that she had used once before, after their trip to the sliding cave and the cheese store. She opened it without a word and stood back in the shadows as the afternoon light flooded in. Eddie stood still and stared at her. It was hard to see her with the daylight blinding his right side.

'What *are* you, Gwerren?' he asked. She stared back at him, blinking. 'You're not—you're not normal, are you?'

She looked at her feet—those curiously energetic rippling feet. 'Do you want me to be normal?'

'Are you . . . a ghost?' He thought that might explain how pale she was; how she couldn't be seen by the cavers.

She laughed. 'Have you ever seen a ghost eat a cad-berries bar?'

'So—what then?' Suddenly he was struck by the urge to pull her out of her world and into his. He grabbed her wrist and tugged her towards the doorway, but she pulled herself out of his grasp and then, in a second, she was gone. She had fled back into the dark so fast that he had barely been able to see the movement. He was still staggering backwards from the recoil of failing to catch her when he realized he was alone.

'Gwerren!' he called, back up the dark cave passage. But only the short reverberation of his own voice returned to him. He stepped back in and along it a little way but then sighed, turned, and walked out to the light instead. As soon as he was clear of it, the door closed behind him and became an impenetrable rock face—just like last time. He sat down and leaned his back up against it. He felt deflated and glum and really wished he hadn't tried to grab her wrist. It was . . . well . . . impolite at best.

And he was still no nearer to knowing what was happening in the caves. Weird stuff. Very weird stuff. He should probably never go back. He'd probably frightened Gwerren off for good anyway. His heart sank at this thought. He really hoped he was wrong. He shook his head, got up, and began to make his way along the steep wooded valley, in the direction of the hilltop path to his cousins' house.

Behind him the rock face shimmered and a crack appeared to one side of it for a few seconds. Then it disappeared and the rock face was smooth once more.

Chapter 10

The day had grown overcast and slightly muggy. Eddie trudged back over the hills and wished over and over that he hadn't had a row with Gwerren. Whatever she was, she was his friend—and he didn't want to lose her. Worse—he didn't think he could go back again for a couple of days. There was a family outing planned with his cousins tomorrow. He checked his watch. Soon he would be back with them all, eating something with oven chips. He would have to escape into Uncle Wilf's room after tea if he was to have any hope of cheering up.

He found one of the many old stone stiles and sat down on the top of it to think—and put off going back to his cousins' a little longer. Why wouldn't Gwerren come out of the caves? Surely she had to come out sooner or later when it was time to go home with Stan? He decided he would ask Stan where

Gwerren and her family lived the next time he saw him. Perhaps he could plan something fun for them both to do outside the caves one day this summer.

He fished out his binoculars and surveyed the hills and valleys that stretched out around him. He watched a large buzzard fending off a smaller hawk, which was divebombing it repeatedly while it perched at the top of an elder tree in a field some way off. The buzzard languidly flapped a large wing at the hawk from time to time, but did not leave its perch. Swinging the lenses around, Eddie noticed movement on the hillside behind the buzzard's tree. He was used to seeing the occasional walker or horse and rider, but the three figures crossing the lower slope, a hundred metres or so below him, had a particular purpose in the way they walked. He quickly trained and refocused his binoculars. Yes. He was right. It was the cavers who had passed them in the passageway. They must be on their way to get that steak pie, walking back over the hills like he did.

He still found it hard to believe that they had not seen him and Gwerren. Eddie slid off the stile and walked swiftly in the same direction as the cavers. Their path did not take him far from his route home, and he had the urge to look at them up close again. Moving downhill across bumpy, ankle-height grass,

Eddie closed the gap quite quickly. The cavers vanished into a small gathering of trees in one of the familiar belly-button dips on the landscape, and Eddie broke into a run, knowing that they would not now glance over a shoulder and spot him.

A few minutes later he entered the shade of the tiny copse and looked around him for clues to where they had gone. He listened hard but did not hear any voices, just the sighing of the wind in the leaves. But he noticed a metallic glint between the trees and walked towards it. A minute later he was surprised to see metal posts and chain link fencing blocking his path. The fenced-off area was no bigger than a medium sized shed, he guessed. Beyond it he could see an earthy well dropping away amid chunks of rock and clods of earth. It hadn't been dug all that recently, but there was a ladder leading down into it and a small mud-spattered generator crouched near the top of the ladder, presumably to power some kind of digging gear. There was a gate in the metal post fencing. On it was a yellow sign which read: WARNING! DANGER OF FALLING. It was padlocked shut, but it wasn't very high. Only up to his shoulder. And the chain link was quite easy to get up. Yes—there was a warning sign—but it didn't actually say KEEP OUT, did it? It couldn't hurt to have a closer look.

Eddie dropped his backpack to the ground along with his binoculars, and anchored his fingers high into the chain link. With a jump, he climbed up the fence and over it. He dropped to the ground on the other side with a thud and stepped cautiously towards the hole. How far down did it go? He walked around to the ladder side and got down on his hands and knees to lean out over it a little way. Below him the blackness of the deep earth snaked up between small rocky outcrops. This was a proper pothole! Not an excavated shaft. It was one of those vertical routes down into cave-land, scoured out by thousands of years of water work. Someone must have found out that it was here, in the tell-tale dip in the land, and begun to dig out the mud and twigs and stuff which had filled it up over the centuries. How far had they got?

Eddie put his hands on the top rung of the ladder and leaned out further. Did he dare to climb down a little way? Yes. He stood, turned, and carefully put his feet on the third rung down, while he gripped the top rung. He was safe enough. It was a sturdy metal ladder, fixed securely to the rock. He had no idea how far down it went, but he only wanted to go a little way, just to look a bit further in, beyond the first ledge of rock which blocked his view. He wished again that he had one of those hats with a torch on the front. He couldn't easily climb and shine a torch at the same time. Six, seven, eight rungs down, his fingers increasingly chilled by the coldness of the metal, he felt the utter stillness of the earth's upper crust fold in around him. The noises from above—birds singing, leaves blowing—faded away. The quiet was compelling. He looked down and saw more fathomless dark beyond the dim grey fringe of the rock he could still make out. With no torch, this far was all he was going to be able to see. He closed his eyes, breathed in the scent of ancient earth. OK. Time to go back up. He moved quickly, watching his hands on the rung in front of him.

Then he shouted out in shock as he was grabbed by the shoulders and hauled off the ladder.

'What the hell do you think you're doing?' The voice was low and annoyed and the hands were strong and gripped his shoulders hard. He was yanked up into the air and set down hard at the side of the ladder top. 'The fence is here for a reason, you silly sod.' He blinked, still gasping with shock, into the face of his captor. It was the fair-haired man from the cave team. His hat was off and Eddie could see that he was the youngest of the trio—probably in his thirties. Behind him stood the other two . . . Dan and John, he remembered, who were heavy-set and older; in their forties or fifties, he thought. They were all giving him looks of iron, but Dan also seemed to be struggling not to grin.

'I-I-I . . . I just wanted to see it,' Eddie spluttered.

'And what do you think would've happened to you if you'd missed your footing and fallen? On your own? No helmet! Not even a ruddy torch! Do they not do brains in your family?'

Eddie looked at his feet. He knew they were right. 'I just wanted to see,' he repeated, sounding as stupid as he felt. The man—Chris, he now remembered—released his grip a little, but still held on to him, steering him back towards the fence.

'Come on,' he said. The gate was ajar now, the padlock hanging open. Eddie was pushed back outside and the cavers followed. Chris turned to snap the padlock shut again. 'Good job we came back,' he said. 'Had a feeling you might do this.'

'You—you knew I was following you?'

'Yeah, we noticed,' said the one called Dan. 'We saw you cannoning down the hill. Thought you might be looking for a bit of adventure. Would've stopped for you, but we had to get on. But then we remembered the way a padlocked fence affects boys, and came back to check.'

'Sorry,' muttered Eddie. He felt his ears go crimson.

'Ah, get off it. You and every other boy who's been through here!' chuckled Dan. 'I keep saying we should make that fence higher.'

'You interested in caving, then?' asked Chris, narrowing his grey eyes and folding his arms.

'Yeah. I love the caves. I—I go into Wookey Hole quite a lot.'

'Then you should know better than to go down a hole on your own,' he said. But then he grinned too. He held out a muddy hand. 'My name's Chris. And this here's Dan—and that's John.' Dan and John nodded and grinned too.

'If you want to go caving, get yourself kitted up properly,' said Chris. 'Get a hat and a torch and some decent boots. And *never* do it on your own, right? You promise?' Eddie nodded.

'We run classes for young cavers—in Wells,' went on Chris. 'You should come along when they start up again in September.'

Eddie sighed and shook his head. 'I'm only here for the summer. Then I'll be back home in Sussex. Don't you do anything in the summer?'

The men looked at each other. 'We do,' said Chris, eventually. 'But not much beginners' stuff. Sorry.'

They were all silent for a few moments. Then Dan said, 'Get your old man to bring you up to the Hunter's Lodge some time. You know—the place up in Priddy? It's where we all meet up. We can ask around—see if anyone's taking out any beginners this month.'

'Yeah,' said Chris. 'Do that. If you're really keen. But for now—go on home.'

Eddie didn't have the heart to explain that his 'old man' was three counties away and far too preoccupied with nursing his wife to think of taking his son to a pub full of cavers. But he was pleased to be asked. Pleased that these men felt some kind of connection with him. He smiled. 'Thanks,' he said. 'Maybe I will. And sorry for being, you know, stupid . . . '

'You're not the first,' said Chris. 'On your way now.'

Eddie turned and headed back out of the copse, reaching the wide open hillside in a couple of minutes. He picked up speed, moving down towards the path that would take him back to the house. It was now half past four and he would probably have to run to make it back for tea.

Auntie Kath was not impressed with the mud all over his trainers and trousers. 'Don't wear those indoors,' she said, pointing to his feet as he stood in

109

the porch. 'Take them off and hand them over. I'll put them in the washing machine. I'm not taking you out all caked with mud tomorrow! Really, I don't see why watching birds should make you so muddy.'

'Are we going somewhere tomorrow?' asked Eddie, pulling off his trainers with what he hoped was an apologetic grin.

'Yes. We're taking Uncle Wilf to visit Cedar View—the rest home. He wants you to go in with him, though heaven knows why. Damon and the twins will just wait in the car, I expect. Then we're leaving him there for the afternoon and going off to tea with a friend of mine and her son. You'll come along with us, once you've helped get Uncle Wilf inside.'

Eddie's heart sank. She really did mean to go ahead with her rest home plan, then. Today was getting worse and worse. First he'd fallen out with Gwerren, then he'd made himself look like an idiot in front of some cavers—and now he'd learned that Auntie Kath really was intent on getting rid of Uncle Wilf.

He went to the bathroom and washed the mud off his hands and face, changed into some fresh clothes and poked his muddy ones into the laundry basket. Then he filled a hot water bottle and took himself downstairs to Uncle Wilf's room.

Uncle Wilf was dozing in his easy chair. Eddie

110

thought his fingers looked bad. Blue and swollen. The room was cold again. He gently lifted the old man's hands and slid the hot water bottle under them, resting it between the gnarled old digits and the man's cardigan-clad chest. Uncle Wilf grunted and snored gently and there was a crackle under the rubber bottle and some-thing fell into his lap. It was an old black and white photo. Uncle Wilf must have been holding it when he fell asleep. Eddie felt slightly guilty, but he picked up the photo and looked at it. It was creased and yellowed with age, and the image on it was dim, taken in poor light. It was a girl. A girl with fair hair and a lovely smile which managed to light up her large eyes even through the darkening of what must surely be several decades. She must have liked the photographer, thought Eddie. Her look was so . . . so special. Could this be the girl that Uncle Wilf had been in love with, way back in the war years?

'You've found Ann then, I see.' Eddie jumped and looked guilty. 'Beautiful, wasn't she?' said Uncle Wilf, pressing his fingers into the hot water bottle and smiling sadly.

'Was she your girlfriend?' asked Eddie, handing back the photo.

'Yes, we were courting,' he replied, collecting the elderly image and turning it fondly in one hand. 'After

111

a fashion. Didn't used to go anywhere much, truth be told. She wasn't keen on meeting people. Never did get to introduce her to my dad and ma. They thought I was making her up!'

'Why would they think that?'

'Ah—they were probably just teasing me. I was a shy lad. The girls in Wells were always teasing me too. That's probably why I loved Ann. She could tease—but never unkind-like. She was lovely to be with. Like a warm bath.'

'So what happened? Why didn't you get married or something?'

Uncle Wilf sighed. 'The war took me away from her. And when I came back, she was gone. Maybe she thought I was dead and found herself someone else. Quite a few people did think that. I was a prisoner for a long time, and even if I could've written to her, I didn't know her address.'

Eddie shook his head. 'But—didn't you try to find her, when you got back?'

'Of course I did. She was the only one I ever wanted. I asked and asked about her, but nobody even said they knew her. I think some of them thought I was daft in the head—shellshocked or something. They said she never existed in the first place. And I had no proof, of course, because none of them ever met her—and the photograph could have been of anyone. We used to meet on the hills in the evening, after dark. None of your hanky-panky, mind—she was a proper lady. A bit strange, but a proper lady. We used to talk about all sorts. Never met another girl like her. Tried—but never did. That's why I'm an old bachelor and come to this.' He looked around him bleakly and Eddie remembered tomorrow's outing.

'Auntie Kath told me about the rest home visit tomorrow. You still want me to come?'

'Oh yes,' he nodded. 'Remember—you're on denture watch!'

'Uncle Wilf,' Eddie began, unsure how to continue, 'I—I think I know what you mean about how some girls can be . . . different.'

Uncle Wilf smiled at him and the hot water bottle glopped musically on his chest. 'You got yourself a sweetheart already?'

'Oh no—nothing like that!' Eddie felt his ears get hot. 'And anyway—it's all gone a bit wrong. I think I've upset her. We argued and she ran off and I don't know if she'll want to see me again.'

'Do you want to see *her* again?'

'Yes—yes I do. She's really cool and . . . she's easy to be with. Like you were saying, she doesn't spend all her time trying to make you feel stupid or anything. And she's really, really different from anyone else I know.'

'Go and see her, then. Say you're sorry. Make it up. Don't ever leave things to chance. That's what I did—I thought I knew how it would all work out, but I was wrong.' He put the photo carefully into his shirt pocket and shook his head. 'Maybe she was just a ghost after all. They say that there *are* ghosts on the Mendip Hills, you know. Ancient hunters—they've been seen running across the hills in the night and then vanishing. And witches too; they say they walk out after dark and stalk young men on their travels. Pale, pale creatures who cling to normal men and try to pull them away from normal life. Maybe they were right.'

Eddie stared at Uncle Wilf, wondering if the old man even knew he was saying this out loud.

'Maybe,' he sighed, 'she was just one of them ghosts. She certainly seemed real enough though. I held her hand and it was warm. She was warm. Yes . . . she *was* warm.' And he closed his eyes and drifted back to sleep, clasping the hot water bottle as if it were the warm hand of his long-lost love.

Eddie felt a lump of sadness move down through his throat. He left the room.

114

Chapter 11

Giggle. Giggle. Squeak. Tickle.

Eddie was deep in a dream. In it he was chasing along the limestone passages of the caves, trying to keep up with Gwerren. He could see the flick of her hair at a turning, the blue light of the glow-thing she carried bouncing off the walls, the edge of her bare heel, but never could he see her completely, or catch her up—although he could hear her occasional giggle echoing back to him.

Giggle. Tickle. Itch. Squeak.

Something was tickling his face. Eddie swiped at his brow and tried to turn over in bed. There was a shriek—two shrieks—and the patter of feet, running away. Eddie sat up, blearily pushing his duvet to his lap and raking his hands through his hair. Damon sniggered from his cabin bed.

'What?' snapped Eddie. He was still feeling

crabby from failing to catch up with Gwerren in his dream.

'Nuffin,' sniggered Damon, returning his attention to a sports magazine.

'Come on, children!' called Auntie Kath from downstairs. 'We need to be going soon. Up you all get!'

Eddie shuffled into the bathroom and opened the mirror fronted cabinet above the sink to get his toothbrush. Of course—today they were going to take Uncle Wilf to visit the council-run rest home in Wells. Then they were off to see the 'family friend'. He wasn't looking forward to either of these expeditions. Viewing Uncle Wilf's possible new home would be depressing and bring up that nasty sense of injustice that he had to battle with every time he thought of the mysteriously spent seventy or eighty thousand pounds and the strange lack of an 'annexe' ever being built. And apparently Auntie Kath's friend had a son of about his age who got on really well with Damon. That didn't bode well. And he'd have to share a car with them all and—WOOOAAAAHH!

Eddie had just glanced up to the mirror on the cabinet door and clocked his face. It was covered in little blobs of glitter gel and stick-on sequin things. *That's* what Damon was sniggering at. His delightful cousins had decided to do a make-up job on him.

Eeeuurgh! He shuddered and tried to wipe it all off, noticing that they'd even managed to get some blue eye-shadow on his eyelids.

Shrieks and giggles outside the bathroom told him that Kayleigh and Chanelle had been stalking him, waiting for the moment of discovery. He pulled open the door to shout at them but they were already halfway down the stairs, squeaking with mirth.

'Nice look, dancing queen,' chortled Damon, leaning round his bedroom door. 'You should try on one of their spangly dresses, shoontya?'

It took ages to wash it all off. He emerged downstairs with a face pink from scrubbing, shooting dark looks at the twins as they ate their cereal. Damon shoved a chocolate spread-laden triangle of toast into his mouth, sideways, and grinned maliciously through it. Staying with his cousins just got worse and worse. Eddie knew he ought to be able to see the funny side of it, but all he wanted was to smack Kayleigh's and Chanelle's smug little faces down into their Shreddies and milk—and then shove Damon's head under the grill for good measure.

Getting Uncle Wilf into the people mover took some time. His arthritis seemed to have worsened dramatically overnight. It often affected his hands, but today his shoulders and arms were all hunched and bunched, and he kept whistling quietly through his teeth with the pain of trying to get moving as Eddie did his best to help. He took the old man's arm and guided him up the step from his room, across the kitchen and into the hallway. 'Is there anything I can do to help?' he asked as Auntie Kath joined them at the door, huffing and tugging at Uncle Wilf's other arm. 'Should I get painkillers or something?'

'He's already had his tablets,' said Auntie Kath. 'Don't fuss over him so—he'll only play up more for attention!'

Eddie didn't know what to say to that. She sounded as if she was talking about a toddler—or a dog.

'A nice steamy warm bath would do it,' grunted Uncle Wilf, trying to get into his outdoor coat. 'One of those a day and I'd be ten years younger. How about it, eh, Kath?'

'Oh, Uncle! You know very well that we'd need to get a hoist fitted in the bathroom to get you in. And then you'd have to get upstairs. Of course—there'll be lots of bathrooms with hoists at Cedar View. I expect you could have a bath every day there. Let's ask, shall we?'

'*Bed* baths daily, certainly,' said the woman in the

pale green tunic. 'We don't want you getting all sticky, do we?'

Uncle Wilf looked into his cup of tea. He, Auntie Kath, Eddie, and the woman in the pale green tunic were sitting in the reception area of Cedar View Rest Home, on high, plastic-covered armchairs. There was a fish tank on a side table, with a few neglected-looking guppies nosing around some fake weed, and a picture on the wall featuring three kittens in a basket of wool with the word 'Mischief' printed under it. A smell of disinfectant and cheap cooking fat filled the air.

'Once a week we could manage a full hot bath, I dare say,' went on the woman in the tunic, whose plastic badge identified her as *Barbara*. 'As long as we have enough trained staff to put your uncle into it and get him out again. If we don't then Health and Safety will not allow it—but we *always* keep our guests clean and tidy. A good hot flannel goes a long way and our staff are all very thorough. He'll be nice and clean.'

'I can flannel meself, thanks,' grunted Uncle Wilf. 'No need for anyone else to rummage around in my unnecessaries.'

'And of course,' went on Barbara, who kept looking at her watch and out of the window, as if expecting someone more important to arrive at any time, 'we will see to it that your uncle gets all his pills, so any discomfort is managed properly.'

'Oh—discomfort,' said Uncle Wilf, lifting his right hand and examining the swollen fingers with a look of mild surprise. *That's* what this is! And there was me thinking it was called "pain".'

'Don't mind him,' said Auntie Kath. 'He's just tired. He's normally very cheerful.'

'All our guests are cheerful,' said the woman in the green tunic. 'We are a very happy band here at Cedar View. We play bingo every day and there's always ice cream on the menu. Now who can say fairer than that?'

'Can I have a look around?' asked Eddie, remembering his promise to Uncle Wilf, to check out the lady guests.

'Well, I can show you all the main lounge,' said the woman, eyeing him doubtfully. 'But not into the private rooms, of course.'

The main lounge was filled with many more high plastic-covered armchairs and the carpet was dark green and orange and very swirly. A television was on, with some kind of DIY show blasting out at high volume. Seven or eight elderly people were there in the high armchairs.

'We have to have it loud,' shouted Barbara. 'Because some of our guests are deaf.'

'What about the ones who *aren't* deaf?' called back Eddie, aghast.

'Don't worry—they soon are,' bawled Uncle Wilf. 'And then everyone's happy.'

Eddie checked out the occupants of the chairs. All but one were old ladies and all but two were asleep. The two that were awake smiled at him and he smiled back. One lady was so very old that he couldn't imagine she would have enough energy to even wink at Uncle Wilf, let alone pursue him amorously along a corridor. The other looked younger and had a crossword puzzle book on her knee, which was encouraging. Uncle Wilf liked puzzles and quiz shows and *Countdown*-type stuff. Then the lady called across to Barbara. 'Nurse! Nurse! My bowels need to move. They need to move *right now*.'

'Yes, Elsie,' called Barbara, in a long-suffering voice. 'We'll get to you in a minute.'

'But . . . right *now*.'

Eddie glanced at Uncle Wilf and saw that he was laughing so hard there were tears coming out of his eyes. He laughed too, turning his head away from poor Elsie—but then a flash of memory came to him: the image in the dark photograph of Uncle Wilf's lost

121

love. The contrast was too awful. Eddie gulped and followed them back out to reception, awash with sadness for Uncle Wilf. Was this to be his home? Could this really be the place he ended his days? With the ever present smell of disinfectant and cheap cooking fat and the plastic on all the seats and the screaming TV and the semi-comatose people?

'Well then, this looks nice, doesn't it, Uncle?' Auntie Kath was saying as they sat down again by the fish tank. 'So we'll leave you to look around with Barbara and come back for you after tea. How's that?'

Eddie had a sudden stab of fear. What if Auntie Kath did not intend for them to come back? What if she was just going to leave him here and never come for him and just send his clothes? Maybe she didn't intend for him to have a choice? His mind began to work fast. He *had* to come up with something which would ensure that they all *would* come back after tea today. But what? What?

Then Eddie did something that he never, ever thought he would do in his entire life. He stole his aunt's purse. He pretended to do up the laces on his newly-washed trainers and, while he was bent over, he sneaked his hand along and lifted the black wallet-style purse out of her handbag, which was propped against the leg of her armchair. He sat up with it tucked into his jumper sleeve, then he leaned back into his own chair and thrust the purse deep down into it, jamming it behind the seat cushion. Now they would *have* to come back. She would realize, later that afternoon, probably while they were at the family friend's place, that she had lost her purse. He would make sure of it. And then he would say she had probably dropped it at Cedar View, and they could look for it when they returned.

'Fine. Fine. Off you go,' Uncle Wilf was saying. 'I can't wait to get back to that show—what was it? Turning Your Perfectly Good Front Room Into A Turkish Bazaar. Do you think we could get that nice girl in dungarees to come and do everything up round here, then?'

'Maybe, Uncle,' said Auntie Kath, sweetly, patting his arm. 'You never know.' She never got his jokes at all—or else she wanted to make people think that he was a bit ga-ga.

Eddie gave Uncle Wilf a hug, and whispered fiercely: 'We'll be back! I won't let her leave you here.'

Uncle Wilf patted his head and smiled. 'You're a good boy,' he said.

The friend seemed nice enough. A lady about the same

age as Auntie Kath, she and her son lived in a large house on the outskirts of a village called Priddy. The name rang a bell with Eddie, but he couldn't remember why. Her son, Callum, was less pleasant. A big boy who was sporty and surly-faced like Damon, he looked Eddie up and down and found him wanting in seconds. He ignored his mother's entreaty to take both boys outside for some football and just left the kitchen and went out to the back garden with Damon in tow, never once looking back. Eddie remained, hovering, in the hallway as the women talked to each other over cups of tea and teased the twins' hair into many little plaits, ready for another disco dancing event. Eventually he sat down by the stairs and encouraged a large tabby cat to come and sit on his lap, while he quietly listened in on the kitchen talk.

'How did he take to it, then?' said Jan, the friend, in the kitchen.

'Oh, not too badly, really. He stayed behind for the afternoon happily enough. It's for the best—although it's very hard.'

Eddie frowned at the cat, which looked back at him, unmoved. She was talking as if it was a done deal. As if there was no choice.

'It *is* a hard thing to decide, but then, he's not even your own flesh and blood, is he? Or even your dad-in-law? He's—what—your uncle-in-law? Nobody would expect you to have to look after him twenty-four hours a day for nothing, for goodness knows how many years.'

Eddie gritted his teeth. Uncle Wilf didn't ask for much—certainly not twenty-four hours a day care! As far as he had seen in the two weeks he'd been staying with them, Auntie Kath simply gave Uncle Wilf three meals a day and changed his bedclothes once a week. Occasionally she cleaned the 'en suite' and put the vacuum cleaner round the thin carpet. Obviously she washed Uncle Wilf's clothes too. Was that twenty-four-hour care? She didn't take him anywhere or read to him or spend any time with him at all. Nor did her children. Uncle Wilf had been delighted when Eddie had first offered to read to him. Eddie had read to his mum at home, during her long illness, and knew how much it meant to her. She had told him, before he was driven away to Somerset, that his reading to her and all the other little things he did for her, was what had helped her to get so much better. Not that she'd *looked* that much better. Her skin was pale and papery and she'd had very little hair left after her treatment.

'I know, I know,' Auntie Kath was saying. 'Keep still, Kayleigh, you've made that plait unravel! Now I'll have to start again.'

'And he must be costing you a fair bit, with all the food and extra hot water and so on,' went on Jan. 'And setting up his annexe and all that.'

Eddie waited for Auntie Kath to explain that those costs had been covered by Uncle Wilf's money but she didn't. She just sighed heavily and said: 'Well, you know, Jan, it's been my Christian duty. But it's been two long years now and I have to think of my children too. He's an old man and he's going to be happier with people of his own age, in a place where they have proper facilities for him. You know—rubber sheets and all that.'

'Oh dear, he's not incontinent too, is he?' sighed Jan.

'Pooh! He wets the bed!' sang out one of the twins.

'Now don't be unkind, sweetheart. Uncle Wilf can't help it!'

Eddie couldn't stand to listen any more. He wanted to storm into the kitchen and shout, 'YOU wet his bed, you witch! And what did you do with his money, eh? What did you do with it?'

But he knew that terrible scenes would follow—probably involving him being sent home. He knew his dad would be cross and his mum would be upset and she just wasn't well enough yet, to take it. He dumped the tabby cat on the floor and went out of the front door.

The garden at the front of the house was quite big, grassy and flat and bordered by low stone walls. It was very quiet, set back from a straight road. He could just about hear shouts from the back garden and the regular thud and ring of a ball hitting a basketball hoop. Eddie felt gloom fold around him like a damp shawl. Everything was going wrong. He had probably lost his friend at Wookey Hole caves and now it looked as if he might lose his friend at Auntie Kath's house as well. He would miss Uncle Wilf a lot. Maybe he could go *with* him to Cedar View for the rest of the summer. He doubted it. And anyway, the thought of Uncle Wilf sitting there with the others, in front of that awful, blaring TV, and being thoroughly sponged down by members of staff—it made him shudder. And then rage. The unfairness of it! If he'd only been left to follow his own plans he would be in his own flat now, probably, being looked in on by a nice warden. Warm and OK and probably even with one of those funny baths that you could open up and step into. He *hated* what Auntie Kath was doing and wished there was some way of stopping her.

'Careful. The wind might change and you'll be stuck like that.'

Eddie jolted out of his unhappy thoughts and spun round. A man was walking across the neighbouring garden, on the far side of the wall. He looked familiar. He was wearing a suit and carrying a briefcase towards his car. He grinned and all at once Eddie realized who it was—it was Chris, the caver who had hauled him out of the pothole yesterday and given him a dressing down.

'You do get around!' said Chris. 'Eddie, isn't it?'

'Yes. Hello again,' said Eddie. 'I—I'm here with my aunt.'

'You're Jan's nephew?' He smiled, looking surprised.

'No—no, I'm Kath's nephew. She's Jan's friend. We've come to see her—me and my cousins.'

'Oh, so that lad trying to demolish the house with a basketball is related to you?'

'Yep.'

'Why aren't you in the back garden, too? Three's a crowd, is it?'

'Yeah,' said Eddie. 'They think I'm a dipstick. And my girl cousins put glittery make-up on my face when I'm asleep.' He wasn't sure why he was saying this. It just seemed to fall out of his mouth.

Chris made a sympathetic face. 'So how long are you staying, for all this family fun?'

'Until I go back to school, probably.' Eddie stared glumly at his shoes. 'My mum's been ill and my dad needs time to make her get better.'

'That must be hard for you,' said Chris. 'So is that why you were wandering around the hills and trespassing on secured potholes yesterday? To get away from your cousins?'

'Pretty much,' admitted Eddie. 'I didn't think I'd see you again. How come you're in a suit? I thought you were a caver.'

Chris laughed. 'I am a caver—but it's not a job! Nobody pays me to go burrowing about in the bowels of the earth, sadly. I have to have a day job too. I'm a lawyer. Dan's a builder and John's a stockbroker.' Eddie blinked, very surprised. 'Lots of professional people go caving,' explained Chris. 'We normally get the caving bug at university and can never quite give it up. I've been a mile underground, holding my breath under a nasty sump with a high court judge before now.' He laughed. 'It's a kind of insanity that can be caught by anyone! Go up the Hunter's Lodge Inn any weekend and you'll find it full of highly qualified madmen, just itching to clamber down a dark hole with a torch.'

'I'd like to go there,' grinned Eddie. 'I've got a kind of season ticket to Wookey Hole caves . . . Stan gave it to me. I can go in whenever I want.'

'Stan, eh? He still there?' said Chris. 'Thought he would've retired by now. Well, you're a lucky lad. Enjoy it. See you around.'

He got into his car and drove away with a smile and a wave. Eddie felt better. None of his problems had gone away, but it was good to talk to someone who kind of understood him. He sighed and went back into the house, just in time for his plan to begin to work.

There was a flurry of anxiety in the kitchen. Auntie Kath had emptied her handbag out on the table and was pawing through the contents. 'No!' she gasped. 'It's definitely not here. Oh no!'

'Check the car. It probably fell out in the footwell or something,' suggested Jan. So Auntie Kath ran outside and searched the car, but found nothing. When she came back in, looking stressed and pink in the face, Eddie went on with Plan A.

'I reckon you must have dropped it at Cedar View,' he said, pushing his hands into his pockets and looking out of the kitchen window to where Damon and Jan's son were now kicking a football repeatedly at the side of a shed.

Auntie Kath considered this. 'Maybe . . . ' She furrowed her brow.

'We can have a look when we go back to get Uncle Wilf,' added Eddie, trying not to grin.

'Well, we weren't going back necessarily,' said Auntie Kath, confirming his fears with breathtaking casualness. 'If he was OK there they were going to keep him overnight.'

'But you didn't tell him that!' The hot retort was out of his mouth before he could stop it. Auntie Kath raised her eyebrows at him. 'I mean . . . he hasn't got his pyjamas or anything.'

'Well, we'll have to go back there now, anyway,' said Auntie Kath. 'I'll phone to see if they've found it.'

'Tell them to try down the backs of seats,' said Eddie, as she pulled out her mobile. 'My dad says that's always where things go missing.'

She got through to Barbara straight away. Nobody had found a purse but, flicking a glance at Eddie, she asked them to check the chairs they'd been sitting on and sure enough, the purse was found.

Eddie was jubilant as they drove back. He might have done something to stop Uncle Wilf being stranded there without warning. Uncle Wilf had the right to decide for himself if Cedar View was for him or not. He shouldn't just be dumped there like an unwanted pet. As soon as they arrived Eddie got out of the car, before Auntie Kath could stop him, and hared across to the ugly whitewashed building and into the reception area. He found Uncle Wilf already waiting. 'Come

131

on!' he urged, taking his hand. 'Get going to the car now—she's going to try to get you to stay overnight.'

Uncle Wilf didn't need telling twice. He got up fast for a man with arthritis and allowed Eddie to lead him to the door. 'Nice meeting you all, can't stay . . .' he called to the reception area as they opened the door. Auntie Kath had just reached it. She looked put out.

'Are you sure you don't want to stay over, Uncle?' she said. 'You can, you know. They said you could.'

'No thanks, Katherine. I've had quite enough fun for one day,' said Uncle Wilf. 'I'll just pop back home with you now, if it's not too much trouble.'

Auntie Kath went to get her purse from reception, her mouth pulled tight like a drawstring PE bag. Eddie got Uncle Wilf into the car—in the seat alongside him. At the back Damon listened to his iPod and sang tunelessly along while Kayleigh and Chanelle giggled over a girl's magazine. As Auntie Kath crunched back across the gravel with her purse and her thwarted hopes, Eddie and Uncle Wilf stared ahead through the windscreen and laughed with relief—and a little horror.

They both knew it wasn't over. But today—today they had won.

Chapter 12

'Gwerren! Gwerren! Where are you? I'm here!' Eddie hated the sound of his voice as it echoed across the Witch's Kitchen. It sounded whiny and upset. Probably because he *felt* whiny and upset. He had just trudged for forty-five minutes in the rain, across the hills, to see her. And she had said, hadn't she, that she would always know when he was there and would come and find him? So many spooky things had happened around Gwerren that he had begun to believe this claim—that she would somehow magically know when he was there.

But now he was rethinking. She was turning out to be *that* kind of girl after all. She had just made that up to sound cool. Or she just meant that someone with a walkie-talkie would radio through when he arrived and her grandad would tell her. Or worse, she was still sulking after their row—even two days later—and wouldn't come out. Eddie sat down on a lump of rock which was sometimes pointed out as the Witch's Dog, because it looked a bit like a petrified Pekinese. He sighed. He missed Gwerren. He hated to think that she might not like him any more. All he had done was try to get her to come outside the caves, for heaven's sake—it wasn't as if a bit of sun was going to kill her! What was she—a vampire?

Come to think of it, she *was* very pale. And she didn't take much to the Star Bar. Maybe she'd been sizing up his jugular vein all week and planning to sink her fangs into his neck. He giggled at this silly thought. She had eaten cheese after all. Vampires weren't big on cheese, as far as he knew—and he had definitely seen her reflection in the pools of water they had visited. Vampires didn't have a reflection, according to horror films.

Maybe she had one of those funny illnesses where she was allergic to daylight. Yes, that could be it. He'd heard of people who had to live indoors with thick curtains pulled shut all day and only come out at night. That made a kind of sense.

He stood up. He'd been here more than ten minutes now and there was no sign of her. Soon the next tour party would come through and the guide would want to know what he was doing here on his own. He turned back towards the cave entrance, but as he did so there was a glimmer of blue light and he caught his breath. A second later Gwerren stepped out of the narrow crack in the rock which was once again visible.

'How do you *do* that?' he murmured.

She shrugged. 'Do what?'

'Come out of solid rock like that!'

'It's not solid.'

'It is! I've just been poking at it for the last ten minutes.'

'Ah. You just have to know how,' she said. She was wearing a white cotton dress which skimmed her knees. It made her look very ghost-like, with the blue light from the orb highlighting its folds.

'I'm sorry,' said Gwerren.

He looked at her, wondering what she meant. Hoping this meant they were OK again.

'I'm sorry I ran away from you,' she said.

'I'm sorry I tried to make you go outside.'

She nodded and smiled and looked down at her dress.

'Are we friends again?' asked Eddie. 'I—I didn't like not being.'

'Yes, of course. We've always been friends. And we always will be, I'm sure. Even when we get cross with each other.'

'Why can't you go outside?' he asked, before he could stop himself.

'I can go outside. Sometimes. I just—didn't want to then.'

'Have you got that light allergy thing then? You know—that illness where you can't go out in the sun?'

She looked up at him in surprise and then seemed to consider. 'Yes,' she said, at length. 'That's it.' But she didn't sound very convinced. Eddie let it go. He wanted to go off on another adventure and forget their quarrel.

'Can we go back to the warm cave and swim?' he asked. 'I've brought my trunks today.'

'No, not today,' said Gwerren. 'There's been too much rain. The water levels are too high. It would be dangerous trying to get there.'

'OK,' he said, disappointed. 'So—the punchbowl cave? Do a bit of sliding?'

'I would like to,' she said, 'but I can't today. I have to go to chapel. It's Sunday. I have to sing.'

'Oh.' Eddie was very surprised. He did not have Gwerren down as from a religious family. 'So—you can't play at all?'

'Not today. I'm really sorry. Can you come back tomorrow?'

'Maybe,' said Eddie. He wasn't sure. There had been talk of some family outing again. He might not be able to get out of it.

'Come when you can,' she said. 'I'll see you soon.' And then she was gone. The blue glow faded and there was nothing to be seen, making him wonder all over again if she was actually a ghost. After all, nobody else had seen her except Stan. None of the guides ever mentioned her.

He trudged back to the cave entrance and found Mick there, checking his torch batteries in readiness for the next tour. 'Hello, Eddie,' said Mick. 'Aren't you going round the wrong way? You should've gone out the other end with Phil.'

'I just wanted to see the Witch's Kitchen again,' said Eddie.

'OK—but don't keep wandering off on your own,' warned Mick. 'It's all right you coming around with us. Stan says you're all right and so you are. But we've still got rules. We have to look after our guests and we could get in a lot of trouble if you're found wandering off on your own where you shouldn't be.' He pressed a button on his radio and told Phil that 'Stan's boy' was here with him. There was a crackly affirmative at the other end.

'Sorry,' said Eddie. 'I'm not usually on my own.

I just like to stay behind sometimes to listen to the caves—without people.'

'Yeah. I know what you mean,' said Mick. 'I've been here for decades and I still like to listen sometimes. You hear some funny things once in a while.'

'What have you heard?' asked Eddie.

'Well once, when I had a small party in chamber nine—it was the weirdest thing! We heard singing.'

'Singing?'

'Yes—like a choir. Singing, away somewhere in the middle of the caves. I thought someone must have a tape recorder on them or something, and be winding us up. But none of them did. There was only about six of us altogether and none of the other tours was running. It was in the low season and very quiet. I said "Come on, own up. Who's having a joke?" But everyone was spooked—you could see it in their eyes. Singing, it was. Made the hairs stand up on my neck, I can tell you. But beautiful. I've always wanted to hear it again.'

'Do you ever *see* anything—or anyone—in the caves?' asked Eddie. 'Like—you know—ghosts? Like maybe a girl ghost?'

Mick laughed and went to open the gate to the second small tour party of the day. 'Nah. Wouldn't mind if I did. But not so far! You coming along with me then?'

Eddie shook his head. Without Gwerren the caves had lost some of their appeal. 'No, I'm going back now. See you another day.'

He trudged back up the steep hillside feeling dejected. He felt better that Gwerren was still his friend—but very disappointed that they'd not been able to play. The walk back across the hills wasn't much fun. A gusty wind blew rain into his face again and again, until the cold water dripped off his nose and tried to creep back into his hood. His hands were red and chilled and he thought longingly of swimming in the warm cave. How he would love to be there now, paddling around with Gwerren.

Back at the house there was even worse to come. Eddie hung up his coat and backpack in the hallway, taking care to get his soggy trainers off on the doormat.

'I didn't think you'd be out long,' observed Auntie Kath, putting her head round the kitchen door. 'It's too wet even for ducks today. It's going to clear up this afternoon though, so you can go out with Damon and my friend, Jan, and her son, Callum, after lunch. It's all arranged. I'll be taking the girls to the dance outfitters in Bath. I'll drop you and Damon off at Jan's on the way.'

'I can just stay here with Uncle Wilf, if you like,' offered Eddie, hopefully. Going anywhere with Damon was bad enough—but Damon *and* a Damon clone was a lot worse.

'No, you go along with Damon. It's not good for you, all this moping about with an old man—or being out on your own all the time.' She disappeared back into the kitchen, not giving him a chance to argue.

'Don't worry, ginger nut,' muttered Damon from the sitting room. 'You can get lost as soon as you like once Mum's gone. Me and Cal don't want you dripping around with your girly binoculars and girly bird books.'

Eddie ignored him. He walked through the kitchen, where Auntie Kath was looking at loads of official papers and bank stuff on the big table, and stepped down into Uncle Wilf's room. He found Uncle Wilf in his usual chair. The TV was off and Uncle Wilf was holding a piece of paper in his fingers. He wasn't looking at it, but off into the middle distance. He jumped when Eddie touched his shoulder.

'What's this?' Eddie leaned over to pick up the paper, which had fallen on to the floor when Uncle Wilf had jumped.

'Nosy,' said Uncle Wilf, taking it back from him. Then he sighed. 'It's the end of the road, Ed. The end of the road. It's the offer of a place at Cedar View. I'm a very lucky man, apparently. It's the last council run home in the area. The state's agreed to pay for my rubber sheets and bingo cards.'

Eddie sank down on to the floor at Uncle Wilf's feet. 'But—but you don't have to go, do you? I mean, it's an *offer*. Not an order!'

The old man sighed and smiled sadly. 'Your aunt's already planning what to do with her garage once she gets it back. I'm not wanted here, Eddie. I have to go.'

'You are wanted here!' cried Eddie. '*I* want you here!'

Uncle Wilf seemed to smile some more, but the smile crumpled into some other emotion. 'And if *you* were here for good, I might make more of a fuss to stay,' he said. 'But you're not. And there's nobody else to stay for. My nephew's all right, when he's around, but he's not going to fight to keep me here. It's just the way it is, Ed. Don't fret about it. It's life.'

Eddie felt assailed by grief and anger and confusion all at once. He wanted to say, 'Well, come and live with me—and my mum and dad—at our home!' But he knew he couldn't. If his dad was struggling to look after his mum so much that Eddie had to go away, then he certainly couldn't take an old man too—an old man that he was not even related to.

'It's not right,' muttered Eddie. 'They shouldn't

141

make you. I'm going to tell her!' But Uncle Wilf caught his arm before he could rush back into the kitchen.

'Come on now, don't be silly,' he said. 'Don't go falling out with your aunt or you might get sent home before they ship me out—and I'd like to have you here still to see me off. Come on, sit up on the bed and tell me what you've been up to. You been back to the caves again? Oh—and did you sort out that squabble with your sweetheart?'

'She's not my sweetheart!' Eddie protested, sitting down on the corner of the bed and leaning on one of the wings of Uncle Wilf's armchair. 'She's my friend. And yes—we're OK now. I saw her this morning, at Wookey Hole, but she didn't have time to play. So I came back.'

'She's a village girl, then?' asked Uncle Wilf, tucking the unwelcome letter into his cardigan pocket.

'Yeah, she must be. Although we only play in the caves. Her grandad works there, you see.'

'Mine was a village girl,' remembered Uncle Wilf, his eyes growing misty. 'Beautiful, she was. You saw the photo, didn't you?'

'Yes. She was beautiful. I wonder what happened to her. You really never heard of her again?'

'No. Not a thing. Maybe she went off with some American soldier. Some of them came out this far, you know. There were some in Bath, I think. She's probably in America with a dozen American grandchildren now. I hope. I want to think she ended up better than I did.'

Uncle Wilf talked on for a while, about the old days. Then he got sleepy, so Eddie left him to doze off and walked back to the kitchen.

Auntie Kath had pulled all her papers together and was putting them in box files. She was on the phone, clutching it in one hand as she put the lid down on one of the boxes. She didn't notice him come in. 'Yes,' she was saying. 'It's fine. You don't have to worry. It's all safe in the high interest account. Well, I know—but it's not going to make any difference to him, is it? Why give it away to the council? It's not as if it was going to get spent on anything else and I say the government ought to pay for him now. He served his country, didn't he? They owe him.'

Eddie stood still, wondering what she was talking about. It seemed to be about Uncle Wilf.

'Look,' said his aunt, her back turned to him. 'What's an old man going to do with that much money, anyway? He can't even get down the road to the corner shop. He's not going to be around much longer anyway, and you can't take it with you . . . '

Eddie was aghast. She *was* talking about Uncle

Wilf! About his *money*. Did that mean there was still some left that she hadn't told him about? He edged back into Uncle Wilf's room and looked at the old man asleep in the chair.

Should he wake him and tell him? Should he shop his aunt for taking Uncle Wilf's money and then turfing him out into council care? Damn right, he should! He gritted his teeth and clenched his fists. He was so angry it was all he could do not to run back into the kitchen and slap his aunt.

'Come on, Eddie. Time to go now.' The object of his fury had finished her phone call and put her head round the door.

'Leave Uncle Wilf to his sleep. Old people like their sleep . . . '

Chapter 13

'Stop! I can't . . . *breathe*!' Eddie's voice came out high and gurgly as he struggled to get the words out past his crushed voicebox. He sounded like a distressed chipmunk.

Damon and Callum just sat on him all the harder, grinding his face into the wet grass.

'Callum! Eddie! Damon! Do stop horsing around,' called Jan from some way down the slope. She had decided that what the boys needed was a good run across the hills in the afternoon sun. She was carrying some rainproof macs in case the clouds returned but the day was bright and warm and steam was rising towards the sky from the drenched earth. They had hiked along the road for half a mile before turning right by a grey stone inn which Eddie had stared at in fascination as they passed. It was called the Hunter's Lodge Inn—wasn't that where all the cavers hung out?

He had asked Jan, who seemed nice enough when she wasn't siding with Auntie Kath over chucking Uncle Wilf into a care home, and she said yes, that was the cavers' haunt. She wouldn't take him in, though.

'You're a little young to be after a pint of beer, aren't you, Eddie?' she had laughed, striding on. 'Go on now, catch up with Damon and Callum. They want you to join in their game.'

And yes, they *had* wanted Eddie to join in their game. The game was called Squash the Ginge and they began to chase him across the hills, shouting out 'Squash the ginge! Squash the ginge!' and as soon as they caught him (which was quite often) they sat on him heavily, bellowing with laughter. It was such fun. For Damon and Callum. Eddie thought he might have a broken rib.

'I mean it,' he wheezed out. 'I can't breathe!'

'So how come you can talk, then, Ginge?' sneered Damon. But he got up because Jan was getting closer now and might be able to see that they were trying to injure him.

'Come on!' shouted Callum. 'Race you to the top of the hill! Last one to the wood's a ginger dipstick!'

'Well, you boys go on over the hill,' puffed Jan, pushing her blonde hair out of her eyes and looking rather pink in the face. 'Have fun! I'm going to go

146

along the valley. I'll meet you at the other end. Don't keep me waiting now!'

Eddie was about to offer to go with her, but she shooed him on before he could say it. 'Go on, Eddie! Don't let them leave you behind. Show them what you've got!' She sounded like a PE teacher. The kind that doesn't notice when there's a blizzard on the football field and you're having an asthma attack. Eddie sighed and ran off in the same direction as Damon and Callum, although he was in no hurry to catch them up. As soon as Jan had walked down out of view he dropped to a walk, watching the two boys ahead of him reach the little wood and vanish among the trees. Eddie moved on warily. They were almost certainly planning to ambush him if he followed them in. He would be best off skirting around the edge of the wood, which was no more than the size of a big garden in another one of those odd belly-button dips on the top of the hill.

But as he reached the trees and began to turn to walk along the edge, Callum suddenly burst out upon him. His face was beetroot red and his eyes were bulging. He looked terrified. 'He's gone! He's gone down!' he shrieked at Eddie. 'He's gone down!'

'What are you talking about?' Eddie stared at the boy, who was capering about like a deranged monkey and pointing and screaming.

'He's gone! He's gone down!'

He grabbed Callum's arm. 'Calm down, you idiot! What are you talking about?'

'Da-Damon! He's just gone down a hole! He fell down it! He's dead! He's *dead*!'

For one moment Eddie, feeling his heart begin to pound, wondered if Callum was winding him up, like he had been all afternoon—but he dismissed this thought as soon as it rose in his head. Callum's voice was filled with genuine fear and shock. Eddie tugged him back towards the trees. 'Come on—show me where he went!'

They ran back into the wood and Callum led the way between the trees and clumps of nettles and low scrub bushes, with a weird, faltering, stumbling step. He was weeping and gasping, 'He's gone! He's dead! He's gone!' Eddie could not hear Damon crying out. This looked bad. Very bad indeed.

They reached the place where Damon had fallen. Callum, with hitching, tearful breaths, leaned over a patch of ivy and brambles, and pulled back a handful of the scrawny vegetation to reveal a yawning dark hole, perhaps a metre and a half across. Eddie peered down it, expecting to see Damon a few feet below, whining and dazed—but all he could see was a rough spiral of rock filled with more blackness, stretching down and down.

'I told you,' sobbed Callum. 'He's gone! He's dead!'

'Shut up!' said Eddie. He took his torch out of his backpack, leaving the bag on the ground, and then sat at the edge of the hole and put a tentative foot across to the far side where a lump of rock formed a step. He anchored his hands in the roots of the vegetation around him and eased down a further two steps onto lower outcrops and then leaned over and shone the torch down.

'Damon!' he called. 'Damon! Can you hear me?'

He heard nothing, but his torch picked out something pale, far down in the gloom. Damon's sweatshirt was pale blue—it was reflecting back in the beam of Eddie's torch.

'Damon!' he called again, louder. 'Are you OK?' He thought he heard a whimper rising up through the still gloom. He reckoned his cousin must be several metres down. It really did not look good.

'I'm going to get Mum,' sniffled Callum, behind Eddie.

'No,' said Eddie, hauling himself back up. 'Your mum won't be able to do anything. I know where we need to go.'

'But I want my *mum*,' wailed Callum. Eddie stood up and looked at him. The boy was white with shock and trembling violently. He was no good to anyone.

'Go on then—get her and bring her back,' said Eddie. 'And then stay here and wait with her. I'm going for help.'

He left his pack and torch behind, knowing he couldn't be weighed down, and ran back to the edge of the wood. He felt a little sick himself. Damon could very well be dying down there. He might have broken his neck. He shivered as he reached the edge of the wood and began to pelt down the grassy hillside, retracing their hike. Until now the caves and the potholes had meant nothing but fun and excitement to him. They felt like friends, in a weird sort of a way, as if they were glad to have him exploring around them. Today's pothole was a very different thing.

Eddie tore along the bridle path and his eyes narrowed as he reached the crest of the hill, searching for the view that would mean help was at hand. The grey building lay in the valley below and he huffed out a gasp of relief. The car park of the Hunter's Lodge Inn was full of mud-spattered cars. It was Sunday afternoon—the busiest time of the week. He *would* get help.

He flung himself down the hill, across the car park, and through the door into the pub. The warmth and the smell of beer and hot pies enveloped him as he burst into the main saloon, which was filled with men of all ages, and a few women too, laughing and talking and now turning to look at the young boy in surprise.

Eddie caught his breath and coughed with exhaustion and then shouted, 'Help! I need your help! My cousin's fallen down a pothole! Please! Help!'

The reaction was immediate. Nobody asked him if he was fooling around. Nobody turned back to their beer or their talk. Several men were already on their feet and one strode across and grabbed him by the shoulders. 'OK, Eddie. Calm down. Where do we need to go?' he said. It was Chris, whom he'd last seen in his lawyer's suit.

'About a mile away, I think,' panted Eddie, now feeling lightheaded with all his exertion and the panic and the heady warmth of the saloon. All around him men were getting into jackets and going off to collect gear from cars, calling to each other to check what they had with them. 'He just went down this hole— it's like a well—in the middle of a little wood on a hill. There was no fence around it or anything. Not like your one that I went down.'

'Whoa! We've gotta newborn!' called out a man, arriving at Chris's side. Eddie recognized him as Dan, the well-built caver he'd met along with Chris.

151

'A newborn?' spluttered Eddie, as Chris turned him round and propelled him back out of the saloon bar.

'A new pothole,' he explained. 'One we've not found before. Doesn't happen more than once in a blue moon. Dan! You got lifelines?' he shouted as Dan opened the back of his Land Rover.

'Yup,' said Dan. 'And a Little Dragon. How long's he been down there?'

'How long?' Chris repeated, still holding on to one of Eddie's shoulders.

Eddie looked at his watch. 'I d-don't know. Half an hour maybe? Maybe forty minutes? His friend went to get his mum. They should be with him. She might have phoned for an ambulance.'

'Right, in you get.' Chris pushed him up into the back seat of Dan's jeep. As Chris got into the passenger seat and Dan started the engine, another caver jumped in the back with Eddie—John, the last of the trio he'd met the other day.

Outside, three more cars were full of cavers and revving up to go. 'Which way, lad?' called back Dan, and Eddie pointed. 'I ran across the hills—it's not a road!'

'No matter. She don't need roads,' said Dan and pulled away fast. Stopping only to open the farm gate that Eddie had scrambled over a few minutes earlier, they sped bumpily over the hill and along the valley and were driving up the next hill to the wood in minutes, a small convoy behind them.

'Won't we need an ambulance?' asked Eddie, peering anxiously ahead to the wood.

'Don't worry,' said Chris. 'They'll have put a call through to the ambulance crew back at the bar. They're used to it. We've got a hotline. Paramedics will be on their way.'

Dan stopped the Land Rover at the edge of the trees and everyone leaped out of it at top speed, gathering up hats and torches and backpacks and canisters and rope.

'Come on, Eddie—show us the way,' called Chris, as other vehicles arrived and more cavers leaped out and gathered their kit.

Eddie hared ahead into the wood, his heart hammering in his chest. What would he find when he got there? Would they be too late? Was Damon already dead?

He heard the shouting before he saw anything. Poor Jan was on her knees at the edge of the hole, bellowing, 'Damon! Damon! Can you hear me?' She looked terrible—white and shaking. 'Oh thank goodness!' she cried when she saw Eddie and Chris, with the other cavers close behind them.

'Is he talking, Jan?' asked Chris, leaning carefully across the hole and shining his torch down.

'He's called up a few times—but he sounds very weak. Oh, what am I going to tell his mother?'

'It's not Callum down there too, then?' Chris was now easing himself down to the first rock ledge, as Eddie had done, in order to shine his torch down properly.

'No, just Damon—my friend's boy. Callum went off to try to get a signal on my mobile and call for help.'

'OK—I need some rope,' said Chris. 'John—Dan—'

And now Eddie found himself ushered back out of the way, with Jan, as the cavers went into action. They were calm and organized, kitting up carefully in spite of the terrible urgency of the situation, and then helping Chris down into the dark well of rock, wearing a hat and a harness attached to a rope which was held steady and paid out carefully by several cavers at the top. It seemed to take for ever for him to disappear from sight, but he kept calling back up to the group at the top.

'I can see him,' came back his muffled, hollow-edged voice. 'About thirty feet down, I reckon. He's conscious. He's moving.' There was some more muffled

154

talking, which Eddie guessed was in Damon's direction. 'Might have a broken arm,' reported Chris, a short while later. 'But his back must be all right. He's trying to get up.' There was more muffled conversation from deep in the earth and then Chris called, 'OK—coming up,' but when he emerged, he was alone, and not dragging a frightened, muddy teenager up with him.

He sat on the edge of the hole and looked worried. 'It's tight—really tight. I don't know if I can get down to him. And if we drop the harness down I don't think he can get it around himself—not with a busted arm. He's pretty cold and disorientated too. We need a search and rescue *monkey*—that's what I keep telling you, eh, Dan?'

The cavers consulted over who was the skinniest, but none of them were any slighter than Chris. 'Alan Blake's a little guy,' said John. 'We can call him up. He's at home in Wells today.'

'It's going to take at least half an hour to get him, though,' sighed Chris. 'This is not good.'

'I can do it,' said Eddie, pushing himself through the crowd of cavers around the hole. 'I'm smaller than Damon. If he went down there, I can.' Damon seemed pretty big to Eddie, but he realized it was a matter of scale to the cavers: Eddie was smaller than average for twelve and Damon was fairly average for thirteen—still smaller than a grown man.

He had expected Chris to immediately claim it was too dangerous for him, but to his surprise the man turned and looked him up and down, speculatively. He glanced back down the hole and then around at the faces of his caving comrades. 'It's not unstable,' he said. 'And we can get him clobbered up and get the harness on him. He could do it.' There were murmurs of concern.

'What if he freaks out? We can't be doing with a panicked kid on top of an injured one,' said one of the cavers.

'He won't freak out,' said Chris. 'He'll be OK, won't you, Eddie?'

Eddie nodded firmly, although he was pretty scared. He could do this.

'We don't know how stable the floor of it is, even if the sides seem solid,' said the same caver. 'It's risky.'

'Yes, but Eddie will be in a harness—and it's riskier to leave that boy down there getting hypothermia,' pointed out Chris. 'At least he can still move about and probably understand what's being said to him now. Much longer and he'll be out cold. Look— I'm the lawyer! I know about risk. I say we get Eddie to help us.'

Others agreed with him: even Jan, who was now hugging Callum to her (he had returned with the phone) and looking stricken and appalled, was nodding. Nobody considered Callum as an option. He was probably too tall and certainly too frightened.

Eddie found himself being kitted out like Chris, with a harness attached to a rope and a helmet with a torchlight attached to the front, which Chris fitted tightly to his head with a strap under his chin. 'Well, you wanted some caving lessons, didn't you?' he grinned. 'Your trainers will be OK—bare hands are best. Don't hurry—take your time—use your footholds and handholds and if you slip we'll pull you up straight away. OK?'

'OK,' said Eddie, trying to keep the shake out of his voice. All he had to do was go down the hole, get the harness round Damon, and get up again. Maybe he'd be able to help Damon up first, though, if there was enough space at the bottom.

Chris echoed this thought. 'If there is room to get him up past you first, that'll help—you can get him to his feet and up a little way before we winch him back. And you have to pull hard, twice, on his rope, when you want us to start winching him up. On *your* rope, if you need us to stop winching you it's one tug; to start winching again, it's two. And shout

157

too—we can hear you.' He looped the spare harness, with another hard hat hooked onto it, across Eddie's chest and one shoulder. Extra rope from the spare harness was also paid out by the cavers, along with Eddie's rope. Chris checked his harness was on properly and then nodded. 'Right—you ready?'

'Yes,' said Eddie and got his legs down over the edge of the hole. He leaned across and found the first rocky ledge as before and then began to make his way further down, the rope from his harness held taut by the cavers at the top, but still paying out as he went on down. His head torch threw light ahead of him, flashing up scattered images of rock and earth and aged plant matter dangling here and there. He tipped his head forward wherever he could and caught sight, sometimes, of Damon's legs or shoulder. He thought he saw movement once, but he was worried by how quiet Damon was. Damon usually grabbed every chance to make an enormous fuss if he was even slightly hurt. Stubbing his toe led to screams and wails that could wake the dead. If he wasn't complaining now, something must be very wrong.

Most of the climb was steady, edging down and down, rocky step by rocky step—but some parts were sheer and difficult to hold and once he slipped and gasped in shock as the rope jarred, tautened, and held him, dangling, until he'd found another handhold or foothold. 'You all right, Eddie?' shouted Chris from what seemed like a mile above him.

'Yeah—I'm OK. You can loosen the rope again,' he called, sounding all right—although his heart seemed to be skittering around in his chest like an escaped animal. If they let go of the rope, he wondered, would he be able to climb back up past that point without help? He wasn't at all sure he could.

It was tight, in places, as Chris had warned. He wondered how Damon had managed to fall so far down. If he had tumbled, pell-mell, through the dark air, he would maybe have been caught up in one of the narrow bottlenecks of rock—perhaps he had—and then slumped further down as he drifted out of consciousness. Eddie wriggled through the last tight gap and landed at the bottom of the well of stone, with a rattle of loose earth, his feet by Damon's shoulder. He crouched down next to him. Damon's eyes were open and he was staring at Eddie in the beam of the head light, as if he was seeing an alien.

'It's OK. It's me—Eddie. You're being rescued,' said Eddie. 'Are you hurt much?'

Damon whimpered and held his right arm across his chest. Even by torchlight Eddie could see that it looked purple and swollen. He thought Chris's guess was probably right.

'Can you get up?'

'It hurts,' croaked Damon.

'But you can sit up? Yes? Because I've got to put this harness on you, so they can pull you back up.'

Damon still stared at him. He didn't move.

'Come on, Damon. Help me out here,' said Eddie and reached to pull him up by his shoulders.

'Getoff! Getoff! Getoff!' shouted Damon, but he did move himself, batting Eddie away with his good arm and then tilting forward and getting, swaying, to his knees. Good. Eddie unhooked the spare harness and got it up his cousin's left arm and over his shoulder. Getting it looped around the right arm was difficult, and Damon kept howling and batting him away, even though he was trying to be careful. At last he managed it, and clipped the harness across Damon's chest. He could feel how cold the boy's skin was just by brushing against his forearm. In the meagre light he could see a blue tinge to his mouth.

'Look,' he said, wrestling with the double lines of rope which were twisting up from both harnesses now. 'You have to climb up just a little way, past this bit,' he slapped his hand against the awkward rock ledge. 'If they try to pull you up from down here,

160

you're going to get stuck against this.' He now put the hard hat on Damon's head, adjusting the chin strap as Chris had done for him, and switching on the little light attached to it.

Damon stared up and gulped. He tried to stand when Eddie dragged him upwards by his left arm, but then his legs sagged and he sank down to his knees again. 'I can't,' he said.

'You can! You have to! It's the only way out. Come on!' Eddie pulled him up again, crouching down and trying to push the boy up from his rib cage, but Eddie's harness rope cut across Damon's bad arm and he shrieked with pain.

Eddie cursed under his breath and then reached for the clip on his chest. He would detach his harness, get his own rope out of the way, and be able to move more freely to get Damon up. He shrugged out of the harness quickly and tucked it, and its attached rope, up above the bottleneck. He would get it and put it back on after Damon had been pulled out.

Now he tried again, and this time Damon also tried a bit harder, probably because Eddie said there were rescue people at the top, with painkillers and stuff. Eddie heaved Damon up, putting his shoulder to the boy's muddy backside and shoving as hard as he could. At last Damon had got past the bottleneck.

Eddie followed him, climbing up past the limestone shelf, and then he reached over Damon's helmeted head and pulled his rope hard, twice. 'OK—he's ready to go!' he yelled. A second later the rope went taut and then Damon was lifted up, turning slowly in the air and groaning with the pain in his arm.

'Look out for rocky bits,' called Eddie. 'Shove yourself past them with your good arm!' He wasn't sure whether Damon paid any attention—and he never got to find out. As he turned to reach for his own harness, which lay against the edge of the rocky bottleneck, the relief of getting Damon up made his head swim. He stumbled sideways and slid back down to the very bottom of the hole. He knocked his elbow hard and was just huffing with pain and getting up again when there was an odd, sticky, slithering sound and the ground beneath him fell away.

Chapter 14

Maybe he shouted out. Maybe he didn't. There was too much going on to know. He was falling, falling, falling, through a storm of earth and plant matter and twigs and soggy clumps of mud and rock, all lit haphazardly by the flailing beam of the torch on his hat as he spun in the blackness.

It was the most shocking thing. The most astonishingly shocking thing. He had just enough time to think that his life was probably going to end very soon before he hit the floor. It knocked the breath out of him, but nothing broke. Incredibly, he had landed on something soft and wet. He hadn't stopped moving yet, though; he was now rolling, more debris rolling and bouncing with him, on his side, over and over, two or three times, before he finally came to rest on a harder surface—rock again. Incredibly, his light was still on. Turning his head to the left he could make out a mass of twigs and leaf litter and strands of muddy old vegetable matter. He had been given a soft landing. This was why he was still alive.

He hurt, though. His shoulder blades, his right hip, his hands, and his left ankle all complained sharply. And as yet he had not drawn breath. The air had been knocked right out of his lungs and only now, with a whistling gurgle, were they attempting to draw it back in. He rolled onto his side despite a twisting pain in his left ankle, which seemed to be jammed under something, and hunched over at an angle, convulsing with the effort to get the air back in. It was as if his airway had simply shut down and sealed itself, never expecting to be needed again—but at last it opened up, with a tearing, sucking sound. Eddie gasped and gasped and gasped until at last he was able to steady his breathing a little. As his head cleared, the screaming death-edge panic juddering through him began to downgrade to simple dreadful fear. Now the pain in his ankle tried to push itself to the top of his problem list.

He wasn't ready to pay it attention just yet, though. He had just plummeted who knew how deep into the bowels of the earth and he had no rope and no harness and no way of communicating with the cavers above. Did they even know, yet, what had happened? Had they seen or heard anything while they were focused on winching Damon up to safety? He felt water now, coursing beneath him, and also in fine spray above him. Beyond the roaring of the frantic blood pressure in his ears, he now made out the hiss of a stream or water-fall, very close by. He must get up and get back to the soft landing area he'd first hit—see if he could shout up to the top. He sat up and then cried out with pain. His ankle really was trapped! He pushed himself up as high as he could, on one elbow, adjusted his hat, which had twisted on his head, so that the light shone straight, and saw that his soft landing wasn't merely twigs and leaves and mud and roots—there was rock in it too. A lot of it. Some of it must have collided with him as he fell, but he'd been too shocked to register that at the time. The biggest problem was one large piece of reddish rock, which was pinning him down by his ankle.

Of course, without the spongy matter underneath it Eddie's ankle would have been pulped. He had been saved by compost. But sticks and smaller rocks were also heaped around the ankle-trapping rock and Eddie could not lean across and shove them away. He tried, even though it hurt so much that he had to shout out and fall back whimpering, like Damon had not so long ago. He sank back down onto his bruised shoulder blades, dazed, and felt, as well as heard, a splash. Water. Yes—and quite a bit of it. He must be lying in the bed of an underground spring—quite a small shallow one. For the first time, he noticed the coldness of it coursing straight through his sweatshirt and jeans. He shuddered. This was not good. Not good at all. He remembered Chris talking about Damon getting cold and shocked. Well, he was cold—and getting a lot colder if he stayed here. And he had every reason to be shocked.

He could not believe that this had happened. Just minutes ago it had been going so well! He had played his part in rescuing his cousin. He had been steady and sensible and . . . Ah. But then he had taken off his harness. It had made sense at the time, but it was a very stupid thing to have done. And he was living proof of this. For now.

A wave of dizziness swept over him and he closed his eyes. He must not panic. He must not. He was used to being underground. He *liked* caves and passages and . . . He opened his eyes again and stared at his knees. They were both now submerged. The water level was rising.

One of the reasons Eddie liked making up silly words to songs was that it was a game he shared with his mum. His mum had a very ready sense of humour and often started it all off.

166

Start spreading manure, was one of her favourites,
in a proper Sinatra voice,

> *I'm weeding today.*
> *I want a nice big cart of it*
> *Manure! Manure!*

> *That stuff on my shoes*
> *It isn't just clay*
> *It's got a whiff of fart to it*
> *Manure! Manure!*

He could see her now, giggling in the garden,
wearing her paint-splashed jeans, her old holey jumper,
and her wellies, digging up the borders and checking he
was keeping at the weeding. This was when she'd had
all her lovely auburn hair and her skin was pink and
normal and her eyes were bright and shiny in the sun.

Even when she got sick she still kept making up
silly songs with him. In hospital they sang '*I want to
test your gla-a-a-a-nds. I want to test your glands*',
Beatles style. Another favourite was '*You know I stand
in line until you think that it is time to stick a needle
in me . . .* ' They even did the harmonies on that one,
until they were laughing too hard to carry on. It was
a brilliant distraction from the illness. Dad joined in

167

sometimes, too. Most of the time. It kept death outside the door, thought Eddie, that's what it did. Outside, walking the corridors, never once thinking it might have a chance in that side-ward where the woman and the boy, and sometimes the man, were all laughing so hard. Passing by.

When the water reached his chin, Eddie started to sing.

'*Eddie threw a party in a deep dark well*
Couldn't keep his rope on so he went and fell
Now I'm sitting in a pit and can't get free
So come and do the ankle-trapping rock with me . . .'

The song came out echoey and weird and he had to make himself grin to make it sound funny. Then he had to shut his mouth, because the water was pouring into it. He tilted his head back and held himself as high as he could, his mouth just a centimetre or two clear of the rushing cold stream. He thought about his mum and dad, in the garden in Sussex; the tall oaks at the end of it; the greenhouse, the climbing frame, the sound of bees in the lavender.

It was only when the water went into his ears and everything went muffled and quiet that he allowed himself to cry and wish them both goodbye.

Chapter 15

Maybe hell isn't where you think it is. Maybe heaven isn't, either. It could be that everyone's got it wrong. Because, when you think of it, up in space, beyond the clouds, the weather, the ozone layer—is *nothing*. Nothing for humans but dark and cold. No air. No life. Nothing. Why is heaven meant to be there?

And yet, the earth is full of heat and life. Even a cave has bats and spiders and rivers of fish running through it. Why put hell here? Why not heaven?

Eddie wasn't given to thinking such deep thoughts about heaven and hell. He wasn't even sure either existed. But now seemed like a good time to ponder on it. After all, he was about to find out.

'Shhh. It's all right—you're safe now. Just rest a while longer.'

Well, it felt nothing like hell. He was wrapped up and warm and lying down on something soft.

169

There was golden and blue light and someone was smoothing his hair. He was dry, too. This must be heaven, then. Although, funnily enough, it still *smelt* like the caves.

Eddie turned over in his bed and sighed comfortably. But something twinged a little. His ankle. He became aware of something wrapped tightly around it. What was that for, then?

Whoa! Suddenly his eyes sprang open and he shot upright. The cave fall! The danger! The rising water! Where *was* he?

Hands clasped his shoulders and a sweet, calm voice spoke. 'It's all right, Eddie. You're quite safe.'

It was a woman he'd never seen before, and yet he immediately liked her face, which was pale and gently lined, with a wide smile and even wider eyes. Her hair was pure white and plaited down one side of her head. She looked as if she was sixty or seventy years old, but it was hard to tell in the soft light. She moved like a much younger woman.

'How are you feeling?' she asked, running her hand over his brow the way his mum did. Behind her concerned face he thought he could make out a ceiling of pale cloth which swooped down from a central point of golden light, like the inside of a circus tent.

'I—I'm OK,' he said. 'Where am I?'

She smiled at him again. 'Where do you think you are?'

Eddie stared at her, with the golden halo of light behind her white hair and her lovely, kind smile, and ventured: 'Heaven?'

Her burst of laughter wasn't very angelic. He felt perplexed and she put her hand over her mouth and shook her head and said, 'I'm sorry, Eddie! Why wouldn't you think that? You did nearly drown, after all. Wren! Wren! Come in! He's awake.'

Before he could even wonder who 'Wren' might be, a small figure had run into the room. 'Gwerren!' exclaimed Eddie. She dashed towards him and stared down at him, gnawing on her lower lip.

'Are you all right?' she asked, at length. 'I—I thought you were dead. I thought I was too late.'

He could see that her eyes were red and puffy and felt quite shocked that he could have made her cry. He just grinned at her and after a while she grinned back.

'Did you find the cavers?' he asked. 'Did you help them to rescue me? Am I in hospital?'

Gwerren shot a look at the woman and they both pulled a slightly troubled face. 'You might as well tell him, Wren,' said the woman. 'There's no pretending now, is there?'

Gwerren sat down on the edge of the bed. 'You're not in hospital,' she said. 'The cavers didn't get to you in time. You were under water when I got through. I had to get your ankle out and then pull you up. I thought you were dead.' She paused for a moment and her mouth puckered a little and Eddie felt a twinge of guilt over what a nasty discovery this would have been for her: her friend's dead body in a submerged cave.

'I got help to bring you here,' she said. 'I probably shouldn't have done that, but you coughed up water and started breathing and I couldn't leave you in the upper caves to die of cold. You had to get to the warm levels. You're in the warm levels now. You're in Cartraethia.'

'Car-tray-thea?' repeated Eddie. 'Where on earth is that?'

'It's not on earth at all,' said Gwerren. 'It's *under* earth.'

Eddie sat up then, despite the woman's concern. He stared at Gwerren. 'You mean—we're still in the caves?'

'Yes. This is my home. On the Stratas. The warm levels. People have lived here for centuries. There have always been people living here.'

Eddie began to understand. Gwerren *was* one of those New Age types after all. She and her family had decided to turn their backs on the modern world and live the simple life in caves, like those Neolithic people whose remains were on display in the museum. They must have made some kind of deal with Stan and the Wookey Hole caves management, so they could move into one of the caves off the main tour trail. Maybe it was some kind of experiment. They did things like that on TV all the time, didn't they? People tried to live on a desert island or in a house from the 1800s and so on . . . why not in caves like Neolithic man?

It certainly looked as if they'd gone to a lot of effort. The room he was in appeared to be made of cloth stretched around a hexagonal wooden frame. The floor was uneven and covered with what looked like animal skins. There was simple furniture fashioned from wood—some carved and planed, some very rustic, still with bark on, some woven from slender twigs and reed-type plants. A ring of stones, layered to about knee height, contained a gently glowing fire and there was a hole in the canopy above it, presumably to draw up any smoke, although there was no smoke in evidence.

'Do you understand what I'm saying?' said Gwerren.

'Yeah, OK,' said Eddie. He swung his legs over the edge of the bed, which was also made of wood and covered with soft woven blankets. He was relieved

173

to find he was wearing his sweatshirt—surprisingly dry—and underpants. His jeans he spied hanging over a wooden rack near the fire. One leg of them had been ripped up to the knee.

'Sorry,' said Gwerren, following his glance. 'We had to rip them to get them past your ankle without doing too much damage. Can he have them back now, Angrid?'

The woman nodded. 'Of course.' She handed them over to Eddie, who put them on carefully over the bandage around his ankle. Gwerren handed him his socks and trainers, now also dry, and he put those on too, wincing a little when his left ankle twinged again.

'Can you walk on it?' asked Angrid. 'We should probably get you on your feet soon—your people will be very worried about you. He must go back Twubuv,' she said to Gwerren.

Gwerren took Eddie's hand and squeezed it, closing her eyes briefly. 'I think he is well enough now,' she said. 'Just go slowly,' she warned as he stood up.

'Can I see your camp?' asked Eddie. 'Before I go? It sounds brilliant.'

'We'll be walking back through it,' said Gwerren, with a smile. 'You can't miss it, unless I blindfold you. Actually I probably *should* blindfold you. It's meant to be secret. Nobody from Twubuv has seen it for decades.'

'Twubuv?' echoed Eddie, as he tried his first tentative step on his left foot.

'Oh—well—that's where you're from. Twubuv. It comes from going "to above".'

Eddie nodded and chuckled. They'd really worked hard to create their own world here. He wondered if they would do it for long. He supposed it was possible that the experiment had been running for all of Gwerren's life. He stepped carefully across what looked like a deerskin rug. His foot was OK to walk on, if he took it gently.

'Come and see then,' said Gwerren, pushing aside a curtain of woven cloth and leading him out of the tented room.

'How many of you live in the camp?' asked Eddie as he followed.

'Quite a few of us,' she said—so he was prepared to see a community of maybe ten or twenty little in-cave tent houses, campfires and so on.

As Eddie stepped out behind Gwerren his mouth dropped like a trapdoor. He gasped and actually grabbed her hand, to be sure she was really there and this wasn't actually a dream. He was standing on a broad ledge with a wooden safety rail, looking out across a cave so large he could not see the far side— and in it was a small town.

Chapter 16

This small town was lit with every colour of the rainbow. Starry orbs of every shade and size were dotted here and there as far as the eye could see, clinging to rocky outcrops and stalactites, creating a wonderland of light which picked out a whole *town* of hexagonal dwellings that seemed to be made from animal skins stretched across wooden frames, set into low rock-wall foundations. The small buildings lined narrow lanes of smooth bedrock which rose and fell, winding through hills and valleys, and along rivers, even beneath waterfalls. There had to be *hundreds* of people down there; he could see some now, walking and running and standing around in groups, some carrying blue orb lights like Gwerren's; others attending to gardens—yes, *gardens*—for there were plants here! Greenery sprang out from the rocks wherever the light was golden, he noticed—and more than half the light *was* golden. The other coloured lights, he now saw, tended to be smaller and clustered here and there like decoration, while the golden lights were large and bathed the whole scene. It was almost like being under the sun!

A wide river ran along the bottom of the cave valley and he could make out people travelling along it in small boats, carrying bundles and packages—even some children paddling along its banks. There were a few larger buildings too, close to the river, maybe two or three storeys high, which were not hexagonal like the small dwellings, but a more standard square shape. He could see that one was a watermill—a large wooden wheel was turning to one side.

Eddie turned to stare at Gwerren, who was looking at him with a nervous grin. 'Well,' she said, 'what do you think of Cartraethia?'

'It's—it's beautiful!' he whispered. He gripped her hand again. 'Is this real? Am I really here?' It occurred to him, with a chill, that the more likely explanation was that he was drowning still, in the cave stream, and this was just a dying hallucination.

'It *is* real! It's as real as your world,' she assured him. 'My people have been living here for hundreds of years.'

'But—but how?' He let go of her and walked to the wooden railing, which he clutched tightly as he peered at the amazing vista below. 'How can you all live here without sunlight? How can that work?'

'We don't need the sun the way you do,' she said, leaning on the railing next to him. 'We have luminobes. These—' she lifted the familiar blue glowing thing out of her pocket, 'they look after us; keep us warm; grow our plants.' She put it into his hands and once again he felt the strange magnetic pulse and dense volume of it, even though it had no weight.

'Luminobes,' he repeated. 'What are they?'

'They're a life form,' she explained. 'A symbiotic life form. They were discovered when our ancestors first fled to the caves, trying to escape the brutal Viking armies. Many Celts fled to Wales, into the mountains, or the far end of Cornwall. Some got across to Ireland—but our people found the caves. They would not have stayed there for long if they hadn't also found luminobes. Far, far down in the deepest caves, where most people were too scared to go, in case they met the devil. Luminobes love us. They love our warmth and energy and the fact we can move around. They grow against the rock, but they can't move around on their own, so we carry them. We give them motion and energy and they give us light and heat.'

'So—you even cook with them?' asked Eddie, marvelling and remembering the red embers in Angrid's house behind them.

Gwerren laughed. 'No! That would kill them! We use coal.'

'Coal?' Eddie couldn't believe, as he stood here absorbing something as astonishing as 'luminobes', that Gwerren had just said 'coal'.

'Oh yes—there are seams of coal all across the Cartraethian Strata, and beyond to Freja and Omnalisk. We trade our coal for minerals and food in the Gam Stratas.'

Eddie shook his head. 'Wait—one thing at a time! First—how can you use coal underground? Doesn't it suck all the air out?'

'No—we have thousands of chimneys!' laughed Gwerren. 'You just fell down one!'

'But how come we never see your smoke up on the top?'

'It doesn't smoke down here much, the way we use it,' said Gwerren. 'The luminobes absorb much of it—they're a bit like your trees, absorbing gases. We don't need to use coal for heat because of the luminobes and the hot springs. Like in the warm cave, remember? We have lots of those. See the steam over there?'

She pointed off to the right and the far end of

179

the enormous cavern where a round pool gave off a pearly cloud of vapour. Eddie could just make out several people bobbing about in it. 'They have them in Freja, too, but we have the best hot pools,' said Gwerren, with pride in her voice.

'These other places you're talking about—Freja and Monalisk?'

'Omnalisk,' she corrected.

'Do you mean to tell me that there is *more* than this?' He swept his hand across the view below them. 'I mean, how many of you live down here?'

'Ummm.' Gwerren appeared to be counting in her head, tilting it to one side. 'Not that many, really—the Stratas stretch across from under South Wales to under Exmoor, across to under Mendips, and then up to under Bath. We think we are about nine thousand in all. Maybe more. There may still be Underners in the northern cavelands too—under Derbyshire and Yorkshire—but we are not connected to those. We hear tell, but we don't know for sure.'

Eddie sat down on the gently sloping rock ledge with a bump, ignoring the complaint from his ankle.

'Nine—*thousand*! You mean to tell me that there are nine *thousand* people living underground—all across Somerset and Devon and South Wales—and nobody up on top *knows*?'

'Well, *you* know,' she said, 'and a few others. Not many, of course, or we'd all be finished. Overners would invade our lives in a matter of weeks if they knew how and hundreds of years of our way of life would be gone for ever. The luminobes help us to block the routes down to our world. They are a magnetic life force, you see; they can create a field that's as solid as rock.'

'Like that day when the cavers went past us?' asked Eddie.

'Yes, you were right. It was a kind of force-field, made by the luminobes. They are stationed at the entry points we need to guard and they hold the field solid there, so no Overners can get through. It takes another luminobe to unlock the field, so we can pass through. The force-field holds the illusion of rock, too. Without it, we would have been discovered by cave divers years and years ago.'

Eddie laughed and stared around him in amazement. 'This is just so—so—I don't know what to say,' he murmured. He got up again. 'Take me down there! Please! I want to see it! I want to see it all!'

Gwerren beamed at him, but she shook her head. 'Not now, Eddie. Angrid is right. You must go Twubuv. Your family will be terribly worried about you.'

Eddie looked at his watch and caught his breath

with the realization that *six* hours had passed. 'Oh *no*! They'll be going nuts!' he said. 'What if they've phoned my mum and dad? Oh no! My mum can't be told I'm missing—she can't! You've got to get me back!'

'It's all right. Calm down! I'll take you now—if you're sure you're all right? It's quite a climb.'

'Yes—yes. I'm fine. Let's go!'

She nodded and glanced back at the little hexagonal house behind them. 'Oh,' said Eddie. 'Yes, let me just thank—Angrid, is it?'

'Yes,' smiled Gwerren. 'She's my great-aunt. She was wanting to meet you one day—but not the way she did.'

Eddie stepped back into the house, enveloped by its warmth and the earthy smell of the little well of fire. Angrid was looking at an old book. She smiled up at him.

'Thank you for looking after me. I have to go now,' said Eddie.

'You can make the journey Twubuv?' she asked, looking at his ankle.

'Yes, I'll be OK. I have to go or my mum and dad will think I'm dead. They can't think that! My mum isn't well enough.'

'You're a good boy,' said Angrid, in an echo of Uncle Wilf the day before. She handed him his hat.

'Will I see you again?' he asked.

'I hope so. Not many Overners are welcome down here, but you are among the few, Eddie. Go on now.'

Gwerren took him along the ledge of rock and up to a cave passage. It seemed her great-aunt lived at the very top of the cave town of Cartraethia. Eddie had so many questions to ask, but it was hard to get them out as he followed Gwerren up and up and up on the steepest climb yet.

'Wha—what do you all live on, down here?' he shouted ahead, as she leaped away from him in the blue glow of her pet luminobe.

'Fish and vegetables mostly,' she called back. 'Deer meat sometimes.'

'Deer meat? How'd you get that?'

'Hunters go Twubuv from time to time, in the night. Your night, to us, is like day. It's so bright when the moon is up. I've been up in your night, sometimes.'

'But don't your hunters get seen?'

'Sometimes,' she laughed. 'People think they're ghosts! It's really funny! But we are pale and we carry little blue lights and then we disappear.'

Eddie couldn't ask more—he was puffing too much—and his ankle was hurting a lot. He was incredibly relieved when Gwerren called back, 'Nearly there. Can you hear them?'

And yes, he could—he could hear a noise like an axe hitting rock.

'They're trying to dig down to you. I will show you a way through,' she said, as he at last caught up with her. 'Sorry, Eddie, but you'll have to take this off.' She indicated the neat bandage on his ankle, revealed by the flapping remains of his jeans. 'You know you can't tell anyone about us, don't you?' she said.

He nodded and undid the bandage, revealing a bruised and rather puffy looking ankle. His clothes had got damp and muddy again. The only clue that he had been looked after in the warm, dry house of an undiscovered subterranean human life form, was that he did not have hypothermia.

He put his hard hat on—astounded that its lamp still worked after everything he'd been through. Gwerren led him round another bend in the passage and he saw light flooding through it from a low oval gap. He crawled towards the gap and realized he was looking across into the well of rock he had climbed down seven hours ago, in the harness. It was filled with light now. Big bright lamps were suspended on ropes. Through the steady ringing of an axe he heard a voice he recognized—Dan—calling down. 'Chris! Come up, mate. You're exhausted. My shift now.'

'No!' called back Chris, a few feet below Eddie's

viewpoint, which was like a window into their world. 'I am not giving up on this! I am not! That boy is lost down there, thanks to me! I am not leaving him.'

Dan abseiled down into view, kicking against the rocks. 'It's not your fault, Chris,' he sighed. 'We all made the call. We saved the first lad—this was just a horrible accident.'

'We shouldn't have let him go! We should have waited for Alan Blake.'

'Yeah—and then the other lad would've fallen through and you'd be blaming yourself for *that*. We still haven't raised Alan in any case.'

Eddie saw there was a little ledge of rock to edge out on to. He did so, wincing at the pain in his ankle. He glanced behind to say 'see you later' to Gwerren, but she was already gone. Behind him, where there had been a clear, if small, passage, was now a pile of rock and roots and the tiniest gap at the top—as if it had all just fallen in. A force-field and illusion provided by a luminobe. Eddie grinned to himself, still amazed. It was the least of the magic he'd seen today. The lamplit ropes were moving in the well of rock and as Eddie crawled out on to the ledge he came face to grimy face with Chris.

Chapter 17

A day later, back at Auntie Kath's, Eddie found the chance to apologize, properly, to Chris.

The caver arrived, along with Dan and John—the key rescuers in yesterday's drama—to have a thank you tea with the family and to pose for photos for the *Wells Journal*. As they waited for the photographer and reporter to arrive, Chris was sober and downcast.

Even though he had done an excellent job of rescuing Damon—who had sprained his wrist and been mildly concussed, it turned out—he was still aghast at losing Eddie for several hours.

They hadn't really talked the night before. Dan and Chris had got him up to the surface quickly, where a paramedic had stretchered him off, despite his protests, to an ambulance waiting at the edge of the trees. As several cavers looked on, the paramedic had checked him over and declared himself astonished. 'I would've thought you were a goner,' he said. 'You should be cold as stone after seven hours down there!'

'I kept warm by climbing back through the gaps,' Eddie fibbed. 'It was the exercise.' He had told the cavers about his soft landing and then that he had located another route upwards which snaked and zigzagged through the earth until it eventually brought him back to meet the pothole he'd first gone down.

'I think some of it fell in behind me, though,' he'd added, for good measure. He knew they had to believe him. How else could he have got back? But he also knew they'd try to find it later, too—they were cavers after all! And they wouldn't be successful. The luminobe would see to that.

Even last night Eddie had noticed how haggard and appalled Chris looked through the thick grime on his face. 'I'm so sorry,' he'd said, several times, until Dan and John led the exhausted man away.

Now he was here, clean and dressed in a shirt and jeans but still looking distracted and troubled. Eddie took him to one side of the sitting room, while Auntie Kath fussed around John and Dan. Damon, who was prostrate on the couch with an enormous bandage around his wrist, lapped up all the attention, with his sisters looking on.

'Chris, I wanted to say sorry,' said Eddie. The

man looked puzzled. 'You put the safety harness on me,' he went on. 'I took it off, because it got in the way when I was trying to get Damon up. It was stupid. I could still have got Damon up if I'd left it on. If I had left it on I wouldn't have fallen further down.'

Chris shook his head. 'Eddie, you have no experience at all of cave rescue. You're twelve years old, for pity's sake. I should never have put you down there.'

'No,' said Eddie, keeping his voice firm. 'Everything you did was right. It was me who messed it up. But I'm all right—and so is Damon—so please don't say sorry any more. You were brilliant—so were all the others. I want to be a cave rescuer one day, just like you.'

Chris grinned for the first time that day. 'You already are, Eddie!'

Then the photographer arrived and set about posing them all around the couch where Damon lay. He made him sit up and put his arm round Eddie, as if he liked him, with the cave rescuers all gathered on either side of them.

'Do you think your cousin's a hero, Damon?' asked the reporter, who had introduced herself as Emma.

'S'pose so,' muttered Damon. He clearly didn't.

'I was just skinny,' said Eddie. 'The rescue monkey. Chris and the others really did the rescuing.'

Then Emma took him off to the kitchen to talk through his amazing escape from a dark, cold death in the caves. This was difficult, because he had to keep up his lie about finding the other way back up, and she was an experienced interviewer and might pick up on it. He focused on the bits that were true—how it felt when he first fell and how it felt when he found the rescuers again.

He also stressed that he had been stupid and taken off his harness, and that was the only reason things went wrong. He was very anxious that Chris would not get blamed.

At last the reporter closed her notebook and went back to the sitting room to congratulate everyone on the happy outcome of their adventure. The cavers sat down and had tea and Chris looked much happier now. When the twins went into an impromptu disco dance for everyone's delight, he grinned across at Eddie. Man and boy bit their lips as Kayleigh and Chanelle informed their audience that they were lost in music (*high kick, shimmy*)—and caught in a trap (*shimmy, shimmy, kick*).

'Did I tell you my daughters are disco dance champions?' Auntie Kath was saying at the front door, as Emma and the photographer tried to edge away. 'Perhaps you could do a special pull-out feature on them?'

Eddie stood up. 'Come and meet Uncle Wilf,' he said to Chris. The man gratefully followed him.

It was good to be in the quiet of Uncle Wilf's room. The old man smiled up at Eddie from his chair. 'This your cave man, then, Eddie?'

'Yes, this is Chris. He saved Damon's life yesterday,' said Eddie. 'And mine too, probably.'

Chris shook Uncle Wilf's hand. Eddie noticed that he took care not to squeeze it.

'You called your mum, yet?' Uncle Wilf asked, as Eddie and Chris perched on the edge of his bed.

'Yes—this morning. She sounds good. Quite OK. Nobody called them last night when I was missing.'

'Just as well,' said Uncle Wilf. 'Would have been a lot of anguish for nothing.'

Eddie knew that Auntie Kath had been far too wrapped up in getting to the hospital to see Damon to think of phoning her brother and his wife while their son was missing. He was very glad of it. Somebody would have, of course, eventually. He was extremely relieved that this had been avoided. But he had related his adventure to his dad, and then his mum, over the phone that morning, because it would come out in the

Wells local paper and might get back to their own local paper too. And anyway, he wanted to hear their voices.

He made it sound like much less of a drama than it had been, of course. More of a slip on some rubble and a bit of a scramble back up. The last thing he wanted was to be forbidden to go off alone again—or to return to the caves. He couldn't wait to get back to the amazing underground world of Gwerren and Angrid and their people.

Chris and Uncle Wilf had fallen into conversation.

'So you live here with Eddie's aunt and cousins, then?' Chris was saying.

'Yes, for nearly two years now,' said Uncle Wilf. 'Not for much longer though.'

'Oh, are you moving?'

'Looks like it,' sighed Uncle Wilf. 'It's probably for the best.'

'It's *not*!' Eddie couldn't help bursting out. Chris looked up at him in surprise. 'He doesn't want to go—they're making him!'

'Eddie, that's enough of that!' said Uncle Wilf, looking embarrassed. 'These things happen. I'm an old man—I don't want to be a burden on your aunt or anyone else. It's best that I go. Now settle down. I want to hear more about your adventures—and this young man's adventures too.'

Eddie bit his lip. He knew he'd spoken out of turn. Chris had only just met Uncle Wilf. It wasn't really on to start ranting about family troubles in front of him. He settled back, disconsolately, on the bed and listened to Chris talking about the caving expeditions he'd done, all over the world. He'd been to China and Ireland and France.

'We mapped some caves in China,' he said. 'Once we were so deep under that we got disorientated. You stay down long enough and you can forget which way is up. But we had lifelines attached, thank goodness. I'll never forget it though—it was like being in deep space. We got horribly cold then too. One of the guys got a bit hypothermic and we had to get the little dragon out for him.'

'Little dragon?' echoed Eddie.

'Yeah—it's a canister gadget which delivers warm oxygen. It's a life saver in some rescues—when someone's well stuck and it takes a long time to get them out. Helps stop hypothermia setting in.'

'Do you take doctors down with you to your rescues?' wondered Uncle Wilf.

'Only if they happen to be cavers too. Most of the time the paramedics wait at the top until we can get the patient to them. It's no good getting anyone down in a tight hole if they don't know about caving—they're likely to end up a casualty themselves. But we're trained to give morphine injections if need be. I've done that a few times. Only cave and mountain rescuers are allowed to do that, by law, outside the medical profession.'

'Well, thank you for getting our boys out,' said Uncle Wilf. He patted Eddie's arm. 'I couldn't be doing without this one for my last week here.'

'Last *week*?' Eddie got up off the bed, aghast. 'Are you only here for one more week?'

'Five days,' said Uncle Wilf. 'Your aunt's not one to let grass grow under her feet.'

'Come on, mate!' Dan had put his head round the door. 'Oh, hello, sir!' he added with a respectful nod at Uncle Wilf. 'Got to be going now,' he added, back to Chris. 'You've got court this afternoon, remember?'

Chris shook hands again with Uncle Wilf and then Eddie saw all three cavers to the front door. Auntie Kath wafted about, simpering at them. Eddie wanted to swat her like a bluebottle.

'See me down to the car,' said Chris, to Eddie. Eddie followed happily enough as John and Dan tried to disentangle themselves from Auntie Kath's rather emotional goodbye. 'What's going on with your uncle, then?' he asked, quietly. 'If it's none of my business, just say so, but you seemed to want to tell me something.'

Eddie looked at him and wondered if it was right to say this to anyone other than Uncle Wilf. But then he opened his mouth and it all came out in a torrent. 'She's making him move into a nursing home after she *promised* she'd take care of him herself! She *promised*.'

Chris nodded and gave a sympathetic look. 'People sometimes don't realize what they're taking on when they offer to look after an elderly relative, you know, Eddie.'

'Fine. So she didn't want to after all. But she didn't have to spend all his money too, did she?'

Chris frowned. 'She spent all his money? What makes you think that?'

'Uncle Wilf told me that he was going to move into sheltered flats. He sold his house so he could pay for that but then my aunt and uncle told him he should come to them and they'd build him an annexe and look after him themselves. So he said yes and he ended up in *there*—in their garage. It's not even heated properly. And he says all his money is gone. And it was at least seventy thousand pounds! She took his money and spent hardly any of it on him.'

Eddie shut his mouth, aware that Chris was staring at him. Maybe he thought he was a dreadful tell-tale, making things up—or maybe he just thought Eddie had no idea about the ways of grown-ups or how much things cost or . . . but by now Dan and John were getting into the car and there was no more time to talk.

Chris clapped Eddie on the shoulder and said, 'OK, it's a lot for you to deal with, I can see that. Take it easy on yourself—sometimes things can work out OK. You never know.'

And then he was in the car and gone and now Eddie had to go back into the house and 'rest' with Damon. He felt flat. Lost. He wanted the caves.

Chapter 18

It was another two days before he could convince Auntie Kath that he was perfectly well enough to go out again. Even then she was much more strict about when he got back. He realized that she had been rather shaken by the events of Sunday afternoon, so he agreed that he would be out for no more than three hours and back for lunch, exactly at 1 p.m.

'And don't you go anywhere near that wood— or any other place that could have hidden potholes,' she said. 'You stay in the fields and don't go too far off. And take Damon's mobile.'

But Damon protested so vigorously at this, that Auntie Kath relented, much to Eddie's relief. The last thing he needed was a phone call from one of Damon's mates in the middle of seeing Gwerren. And in any case, there was no way there would be a signal in the caves.

He didn't feel too bad about disregarding his aunt's wishes. There was no way he was going off anywhere near uncharted potholes. He wanted to get back to the caves and find Gwerren, that's all—maybe see Cartraethia again. That would be fantastic.

He made it to the caves by opening time, at 10 a.m.

'Haven't you had enough?' laughed Mick, when he saw him there. He must have heard the news, or seen it in the *Wells Journal*. The story had taken up the whole of page five, and there had been a little bit about it on the front page too.

Eddie shrugged. 'Guess not,' he said.

'Well, you're safe enough in here,' said Mick. 'Oi, Stan,' he called down the path. Stan was walking up towards them in the warm morning sun. 'You want to take charge of boy wonder, here?'

'Righto,' said Stan. 'Good to see you again, Eddie, none the worse for wear. You can help me do the tour check.' One of the guides always did a check of the cave tour route before the first tour of the day, making sure the lights were working and that none of the chambers had flooded, which did happen, although quite rarely.

Eddie stared at Stan as they descended the steps into the Witch's Kitchen. Stan *knew*.

'So—what did you think of Gwerren's world?' asked Stan, with a smile.

'It's—it's amazing,' said Eddie. 'You've seen it too, haven't you?'

'Oh yes,' he said. 'It's the eighth wonder of the world—if the world only knew it! But they mustn't ever know it, Eddie. You do understand that, don't you?'

Eddie nodded. 'And you're a kind of guard for them, up here?'

'Well, yes, of sorts. But they manage to guard themselves pretty well. I'm more of a connection between their world and ours. I keep them informed of anything they need to know—like big floods or storms or house building projects.'

'House building projects?'

'Well, yes—anything that involves digging and messing around with the earth. It can have effects down in the Stratas.'

'Do they ever come up and check out our world themselves?' Eddie thought he'd love to show Gwerren around the hills and villages.

'Only at night, usually to hunt,' said Stan. 'They can't take direct sunlight—their skin and eyes aren't meant for it. A few of the Strata people have moved Twubuv. They're normally taken for albinos. In the caves, in luminobe light, their eyes are big and violet or silvery grey, but in daylight they look pink and their skin is almost transparent. They have to cover up a lot. They haven't needed any protection from the sun, you see, not for centuries. Most go back home after a while.'

Stan left him in the Witch's Kitchen, as usual, and two minutes later Gwerren arrived, with her luminobe glowing at her shoulder. They went to the sliding cave and for half an hour did nothing more than whoosh up and down it, until at last they got tired and sat down, their legs dangling over the edge of the huge stone basin.

'I didn't know for sure that you'd come back,' admitted Gwerren. 'After all, the caves nearly killed you.'

'No—*I* nearly killed me. The caves didn't care either way,' Eddie reminded her. 'And anyway, if I hadn't fallen through, you might never have taken me to your home.'

She smiled. 'Oh, I would. Sooner or later.'

He stared at her. 'Would you?'

'My great-aunt likes you.'

'I like her,' said Eddie. 'When can we go back to your town?'

'Another time,' said Gwerren. 'It takes a while

to get there and if you've got to be back for lunch, you'll be late.'

'I don't want to go back,' sighed Eddie. 'I hate it there.'

'But what about your Uncle Wilf? You like him, don't you?'

'Yes—but that's just it. He's being sent away.' Eddie told Gwerren the whole story about Uncle Wilf and how Auntie Kath was cheating him out of his money. He told her about the phone conversation he'd overheard and how he was raging about it, but couldn't stand up to his aunt for Uncle Wilf because of his worry about being sent home and upsetting his mum and making her unwell.

'That's all very hard,' said Gwerren, when he'd finished. Then, unexpectedly, she added: 'What's Uncle Wilf's surname?'

'Um . . . Harrison. Yes—he's called Wilfred Harrison. He was a soldier in the Second World War, you know. And a prisoner in the German camps for a year! It was really sad because he came back after the war to find his girlfriend and she was gone. That's why he never married and why he's ended up with Auntie Kath and Uncle John. Not for much longer, though.'

Gwerren studied her fingers thoughtfully. 'Did he look for his girlfriend? Or did he just give up?'

'He says he looked, and showed people her photo and all that. But nobody remembered her. They reckoned he was making it up—that the war had made him a bit bonkers.'

'And what was her name—the girlfriend?'

'Um . . . something ordinary . . . like Jane or Ann.'

Gwerren stood up and stared at him. Colour seemed to flush through her skin, even in the pale blue light of the luminobe. 'We have to rescue him,' she said.

'You what?'

'We have to rescue him! It's no good sitting here moaning about how unfair it all is. We have to do something!'

Eddie shook his head, feeling a tingle of something like excitement rising over his skin. 'But—where would we take him?'

'Where do you think?' said Gwerren. 'Cartraethia.'

Eddie gaped at her. The idea was astonishing. But . . . he thought of the beautiful cave town with its warm steamy pools and its undulating river. He thought of the lovely hexagonal houses and the gentle glow of the luminobes. He had thought he was in heaven. Maybe Uncle Wilf would think that too.

'Would your people let him come?'

'Yes,' said Gwerren. 'Sometimes we do. Wilfred Harrison will be welcome.'

Eddie bit his lip and thought hard. 'OK—we haven't got much time to make a plan,' he said. 'He goes to Cedar View on Saturday morning. Auntie Kath's already packing up his stuff. We have to rescue him before he goes, because it'll be a lot harder from the rest home. They'll have security alarms and stuff.'

'It'll have to be done at night—if I am to help you,' she said. 'And I think we may have to steal something.'

Eddie blinked. Again? He thought his thieving career had begun and ended with Auntie Kath's purse.

'Steal what?'

'One of the wheelchairs from Mick's store, at the cave mouth. Wilfred will never be able to walk all the way over the hills like you do.'

Eddie grimaced. 'No—but I couldn't push him over them either. How can we do this?' He sighed, dejected. 'We can't pull this off.'

'Edward Villier, I am surprised at you!' she said, and gave him a sharp look. 'You are the boy who's escaped death in a collapsed cave system—surely getting one old man to Cartraethia is not beyond you!'

Eddie nodded. Then nodded again, more firmly. The vague tingling suddenly surged up through him in a determined wave. 'You're right. It's not! Give me some more thinking time—and make sure you're free on Friday night.'

Of course it was not simple. Not simple at all. Eddie was lost in concentration throughout lunch, absent-mindedly forking spaghetti hoops into his mouth in the midst of Damon whining about his sprained wrist and Kayleigh and Chanelle singing and giggling and talking about yet another disco dancing event later that week.

How could he do it? How could he get an old man, who couldn't walk far, from the flat outskirts of Wells through the hills and gorges of the Mendips and into Wookey Hole caves? Without being noticed? He knew it must be possible—it must. It was just a puzzle that had to be solved—and fast. It was Wednesday and the escape had to happen before Saturday dawned.

And even once he'd worked out how—what would Uncle Wilf do? Would he go along with it? Or would he come over all grown-up and sensible and insist on staying put and going meekly off to Cedar View, even though he knew he would be miserable there?

Eddie thought about telling him everything—the whole story about Gwerren and the hidden civilization in the Stratas. But it sounded like a fairy tale. You really had to see it to believe it. Maybe he could make up something else—say it was an outing to a special late night event at the caves. Say he wanted to get Uncle Wilf out with him, just once, before it was too late. This might be the way. Before then, though, there was still a lot of planning to do. He would see Gwerren again tomorrow morning and talk it through further and work and work at it in his head until they had a plan.

He finished his lunch, excused himself from the table, and went in to see Uncle Wilf. The old man was standing looking into a battered leather case which lay open on his bed. Around him there were neat piles of clothes and two other, newer cases, half filled with trousers and shirts and woollens. Eddie sighed. 'How's it going?' he asked. Uncle Wilf looked up and smiled at him, sadly.

'Aah, you know. It's going. Never knew I had so much stuff.' He indicated a pile of books and pictures and small boxes and trinkets on the far end of the bed. Inside the case were more of the same. 'Can't take it all,' he added. 'There are rules about how much of your stuff you can take with you. You get three drawers and the top of the chest and that's it. You're not allowed to put things on the windowsill.'

Eddie stared at all his stuff, and the small amount in his old case. 'Is this all you're taking then?' he asked.

'Looks like it. They don't like clutter at Cedar View. I'll be leaving that lot here,' he waved at the stuff on the end of the bed. 'It'll be in the junk shop next week, I expect. Have a look—see if there's anything you want.'

Eddie couldn't bring himself to paw through those bits and pieces. It seemed rude. He sat down in Uncle Wilf's chair and found the old photo of the lost love resting on one arm. He picked it up and studied it again. He shivered. It was sad. But the situation now was sadder still. He had to do something.

'Uncle Wilf, do you fancy coming out with me on Friday night?' he asked, putting the photo down.

'What are you on about?' laughed Uncle Wilf, still fiddling with his old case and its contents.

'Just for a laugh. Just because—we can. If I can get transport—would you just come out with me?'

'Your aunt will never allow it,' he observed, although his voice was amused.

'No, she won't. Not if she knows. But you're a grown-up—do you want to be told what to do by her, right until you go?' Eddie held his breath, getting up to face the old man. It was a cheeky way to talk to Uncle Wilf.

But Uncle Wilf was laughing. 'If you can arrange it, lad, you go right ahead! I haven't had a night out in two years or more. I don't imagine there'll be many after this weekend, either. Go on. Surprise me. But don't worry if it doesn't work out, eh? It's not easy to get an old codger like me out the door and on the town.' He grinned at Eddie, clearly thinking it was all a bit of a joke.

'Friday night then,' said Eddie. 'It will be quite late. Don't get undressed and in bed, will you?'

'Sure—sure thing,' nodded Uncle Wilf, still smiling, but returning his attention to his case.

'The problem is,' he told Gwerren the next day, as they snacked on Cheddar cheese in the cave store, 'once he's disappeared they'll call the police in and all that—and they'll probably find out that he was seen trundling off down the road with a boy with ginger hair. They'll find out it was me.'

'And me,' said Gwerren. 'I'll be with you.'

'Will you?' Eddie was startled. 'You'll come that far away from the caves?'

'Yes,' she said. 'It'll be fine at night. And anyway, there's no way I'm missing out on this!'

Eddie grinned. 'So—maybe we need a disguise. *You* certainly will. If anyone sees you out in the moonlight they'll think you're a ghost. And another thing, even if we do manage to steal—I mean *borrow*—the

206

wheelchair from Mick's hut, how am I supposed to get it all the way home, over the hills, without being noticed?'

'You don't need to do that,' she said. 'Tell me where to come and I will bring it.'

'I think we could get as far as the corner shop.' Eddie rubbed his face with frustration. 'Uncle Wilf could make it that far, then you could meet us there. The hill walk starts just over the road. But what if we get seen?'

'We won't get seen,' she said.

'How can you know that?'

'I will see to it that the streetlights go out.'

Eddie gaped at her. 'You can do that?'

'Oh yes. We know where all the underground cables for the lamps run. It's very easy to shut them off. I'll do it just before I come with the wheelchair.'

'O-K . . . ' Eddie absorbed this and gave Gwerren a look of renewed admiration. She never stopped surprising him.

Another problem was solved by way of the post. A card had arrived for Eddie when he got back for lunch, from his mum and dad. It was sparkly and carried the words WELL DONE! on the front. Inside, his mother's curly handwriting exclaimed, '*We are so proud of you, Eddie! You saved Damon's life! Not long now, and we will come to collect you. Dad will call Auntie Kath soon and let her know when. Here is some more pocket money to keep you going. Lots of love MUM (& DAD). PS. I am much, much better and can't wait to see you!*'

Enclosed was £20. As he stared at the note, Eddie felt that tingling surge of excitement again. He knew exactly how he was going to spend this money. On a taxi.

'So, good news from home, love?' asked Auntie Kath, as Damon tried to snatch the twenty out of Eddie's fingers.

'Yeah—Mum's much better,' said Eddie.

'That's good then. You'll probably be heading off home soon. The house will be quite empty, what with you and Uncle Wilf heading off.' She looked very smug as she said this. Eddie stopped himself looking at her before his anger could be seen on his face. He tucked the money in his pocket.

'Mum, where's my purple leotard?' said Kayleigh, munching on a choc ice, having eaten next to nothing of her beans on toast. 'I need it for tomorrow night.'

'Oh, yes. And it needs more bugle beads on the shoulder straps,' said Auntie Kath. 'Bring me my box. You've got to sparkle!'

'Oh, not *another* drippy disco dance night,' whined Damon. 'I'm not comin' this time. I got a busted arm, remember?'

'Of course you're coming,' said Auntie Kath. 'We all are. It's the last of the championship heats tonight and we all need to support the girls.'

Damon groaned and rolled his eyes as Kayleigh ran off for the box. She dragged it back in—it was a large chest full of disco accessories and beads and sequins and sewing stuff. Chanelle then ran off to get a smaller box which contained their disco dance make-up and hair gear. Auntie Kath cleared the lunch things away and Eddie offered to stack them in the dishwasher, while the girls opened up the boxes and spread their contents across the table. Soon the room looked as if it had been hit with some kind of sequin storm. Glittery outfits were brought in to be checked over and all manner of twinkly make-up, hair bands, jewellery, ankle warmers, dance shoes, and twirly batons soon dripped off every surface.

As Eddie put the powder in, shut the dishwasher and pressed the start button, he began to beam to himself. He had just come up with a proper plan. Uncle Wilf *was* going to be rescued. Now he knew how to do it!

Chapter 19

Stealing the wheelchair was easy, although it felt very bad. Eddie simply hung back as the first tour of the day went into the caves with Mick.

'I'm waiting for Stan,' he told the cave manager and it was true enough. Stan would be along in a few minutes.

As soon as the tour party had disappeared into the gloom Eddie opened the door of the guides' supply hut. This was filled with torches and batteries and first aid stuff, a fire extinguisher, some wellington boots, and a couple of stools, along with some boxes of tea bags, a kettle, some rather manky looking milk in a carton, and—most importantly—the emergency fold-out wheelchair, leaning up against one wall. Eddie seized it and shook it free from the wellingtons and the back leg of a stool, and hauled it out of the shed. He found he was sweating profusely with guilt, expecting to be caught out at any moment. Not even Stan knew about the plan he and Gwerren had hatched, as far as he knew, so he could get into real trouble here.

He had pressed Gwerren again about whether her people would really welcome a stranger from Twubuv, and she had said it would be fine. But then she'd bitten her lip and added, 'In any case, once he's there, he's there. If we ask first they *might* say no, so it's better that we just do it. Once he is there he *will* be welcome. Trust me.'

This had made him feel quite uneasy, but Gwerren insisted that everything would be all right. And what other choice was there? None. Apart from letting poor Uncle Wilf be driven off on Saturday morning to a life of plastic covered chairs, TV at full volume, and old ladies shouting about their bowels. Eddie had discovered that he even had to share a room with another old man that he'd never met.

Now he wrestled the folded wheelchair across to the tarmac slope at the cave entrance. Peering down the path he could see more visitors ambling up from the car park. He quickly turned round and wheeled the chair, which perambulated along even when folded, into the caves. It was tricky getting it down the first set of steps to the Witch's Kitchen, but as soon as he

211

reached the bottom Gwerren appeared in a flicker of luminobe light and seized the contraption from him.

'Well done!' she said. 'I'll see you and Wilfred at the end of the road, by the shop, at an hour past midnight.'

Eddie wasn't sure how she would know. She never wore a watch. He would just have to trust her.

He had to run to get back home. He wasn't supposed to be out for long. He'd promised to be back by 11 a.m., because Auntie Kath wanted to drive them all into Wells for a pizza restaurant lunch. Now that Damon was acting quite normally again (he'd gone back to being as snidey and bullying as ever towards Eddie, life saved or not), she had decided a celebration was in order and pizza was his favourite. Or maybe it was because she was about to get rid of Uncle Wilf, thought Eddie, that she was so very cheery. She picked up some brochures for holidays in the Maldives from a travel agent's on the way to the pizza place.

He didn't enjoy the pizza lunch much. He was too excited to eat, and besides, he had to listen to the twins prattling on non-stop about the other competitors in tonight's dance event. 'Kelly Marriott's got fat,' snickered Kayleigh. 'And she's wearing pink. She looks like a pig.'

'Hmmm,' said Auntie Kath, 'well, you two are lovely and sleek. I wouldn't allow it any other way.

It's not nice to have to watch someone dancing when they look like something on special offer at Tesco's meat counter.'

'Tamara Wilkins is singing the song that *I* wanted to sing,' pouted Chanelle.

'But she won't sound anything like as lovely as you would,' comforted her mother. 'When you open your mouth and sing—it just makes me cry!'

'Me too,' said Damon, through a mouthful of garlic bread. Eddie suppressed a laugh and Damon actually made eye contact with him, bringing him into the joke. Wonder of wonders!

On the way back home Eddie saw the poster for that night's event as they drove past. It was covered in hand-drawn spangles and stars and read:

DANCING ALL OVER THE WORLD
Come and compete at Street Dance,
Modern Jazz, Tap, and Disco
From eight to late!
Ages 7 to adult.
Senior's ballroom section.

He smiled.

* * *

Kayleigh and Chanelle won first prize in the Disco section, but only came second over all, much to Auntie Kath's disgust.

'You could see it was just because that seven year old was cute,' she muttered as they got out of the car back at the house, at getting on for 11 p.m. 'She really couldn't tap dance to save her life. Her technical performance was totally lacking, but she had those little blonde curls, of course, and looks is all that seems to matter to *some* people!' Auntie Kath seemed to have forgotten how long she had spent plaiting silver strands into her daughters' hair, applying careful make-up and stitching bugle beads and sequins onto their outfits.

'And honestly! The *fuss* when you accidentally hit her nose with your baton, Kayleigh!' went on Auntie Kath, letting them into the house. 'Anyone would think you'd deliberately tried to knock her out. And the blood will come out of her costume if they soak it. I told them that.'

'I truly never meant to hit her.' Kayleigh's glitter-lined eyes were wide with innocence. 'I was saying congratulations and giving her a kiss on the cheek— my baton just got in the way.'

'Well, I saw the looks on the faces of the judges when she started carrying on so! I think she bled into her trophy deliberately, just for effect. Her mother put her up to it. Dreadful, pushy stage mother, she was. The look on those judges' faces said it all—"*we made the wrong decision*". But what can you do?'

It took twenty minutes to get the twins cleansed of all the make-up, hair gel, and disco dust. Eddie was meant to be getting himself to bed, but he offered to help tidy up some of their costume stuff. He took the big costume and accessories box back out to the hallway cupboard and rummaged around in it before closing the lid. Then he helpfully collected the make-up box. He had a quick rifle through that too. Damon had slunk up to his room and nobody else was around to notice him. Good.

Before he followed his cousin upstairs, Eddie looked in on Uncle Wilf. The old man was asleep on top of his bed, with a spare blanket pulled over him. Eddie was pleased to see that he was still dressed. He had obviously taken him at his word about going out somewhere and hadn't got himself ready for bed yet. Eddie hoped his aunt would not check in on him and get him to go to bed properly. He suspected she wouldn't bother. It wasn't her habit to look in on Uncle Wilf too often. And she had packed all the belongings he was allowed to take to Cedar View with him much earlier that evening, before they'd all gone out to the dance contest.

In a few hours he would be out of her life. But not in quite the way she was expecting.

Eddie got himself to bed quickly and lay staring up at the ceiling, willing his heartbeat to slow down and his brain to stop whirring. He was only ninety minutes away from the rendezvous with Gwerren. Could they really do this? Could they carry it off? He had programmed his watch to beep quietly at quarter to one. Now he really needed to get some rest. He closed his eyes and managed some kind of drifting slumber, but in no time at all his watch beeped and he clapped his hand to it, shutting off the alarm before it could get to a second beep. He could not risk waking Damon.

He got up, still fully clothed, and slipped his feet into his trainers. He left the room in silence, feeling his way along the landing. Normally there would have been some light shining through the landing window, but not tonight. Outside all was dark—the street lamps had been switched off. He grinned to himself. Gwerren had been as good as her word. Now—to get safely downstairs and on with the plan. He had rehearsed this again and again in his head. Now was the time to find out if it would work.

He crept down the stairs, creaking the treads a couple of times and catching his breath, scared that his heartbeat could be heard, thundering through the

216

quiet house like a pneumatic drill. Nobody else stirred. He really might be able to do this! Then—horror-struck—he froze, as he heard a door open upstairs and saw a shaft of light fall across the landing. He shrank against the wall, halfway down the stairs, and held his breath. He recognized his aunt's heavy tread across the landing. Was she coming out to investigate the creaking staircase? He felt goose bumps rise up across his arms and the back of his neck, and he closed his eyes tight, gulping. Then he heard the click of the pull switch in the bathroom, and the door closing. Running water. The toilet flushing. Then the click of the pull switch again, the door opening and the returning thud of his aunt's footsteps, before the sweep of her bedroom door closing, the complaint from her mattress springs as she got back into bed and finally, the click of her lamp being switched off. For two minutes he stood in the silence, calming himself down with slow, steady breathing—fighting the urge to give in and scurry back to bed. No! he told himself. Don't be such a wimp. Get yourself together. Uncle Wilf's happiness rests on you!

At the foot of the stairs he grabbed a warm fleece from the coat hooks and his backpack which he had stashed underneath it. The backpack was quite full. He rested it by the door and put the fleece on.

Now he walked through the kitchen and opened Uncle Wilf's door. He had expected to find him asleep and was very surprised to see him sitting up in his armchair. Uncle Wilf looked around at him with a bemused smile. 'I had given up on you,' he said.

'Well, I'm here,' said Eddie. 'You still want to come out with me?'

Uncle Wilf tilted his head to one side. 'Is it an adventure?' he asked and in the dim lamplight his face looked much younger and Eddie could see the boy he once had been.

'Oh yes. It's definitely an adventure. Will you come with me?'

'My last adventure,' said Uncle Wilf. 'Why not?' And he got to his feet quite steadily. He shrugged into his outdoor coat and a scarf. Eddie handed him his old waxed cotton hat.

'Keep it pulled down low,' he said. 'We don't want to be seen.'

He grabbed the small battered case, with the most precious of the old man's belongings in it, off the bed. Uncle Wilf glanced at him, questioningly, but did not say anything. At the front door Eddie picked up his backpack and the key which hung on a hook by the mirror. He unlatched the door and put the key in his jeans pocket. So far so good. Everything in the house was still. They stepped outside into the cool night air and Eddie closed the door behind them as quietly as he could.

They walked along the grass beside the path, Eddie holding Wilf's arm with his free hand, to guide and steady him. It was very dark without the street lamps. Eddie reckoned they were all out for at least a mile or two around this road. In the distance the main lights of Wells glowed pale orange, but it was certainly not enough to light the two fugitives as they stole down the pavement towards the corner shop.

'It probably isn't going to work, whatever you have planned,' said Uncle Wilf, softly, behind him. 'But I will never forget you for doing it, Eddie. For trying. Nobody else would bother. Don't be too upset if it doesn't work out, will you?'

'I won't be,' promised Eddie, 'because it *will* work out. Just you see. Now—here's my friend.'

Gwerren stepped out of the dark with just the faintest beam of blue from her luminobe to light her smiling face. She shook Uncle Wilf's hand. She seemed thrilled to see him. And Eddie was thrilled to see *her*. It was amazing to look at her here, real and actually here, in the normal world. 'You did the lights—it's brilliant!' he whispered.

'Well, it's the opposite of brilliant,' she chuckled.

'Mr Harrison, would you mind taking a seat?' And now she turned round and moved the wheelchair forward. It was quite a good one, with thick rubber wheels which made no sound at all. It didn't even creak when Uncle Wilf, shaking his head in amazement, settled into it. Eddie gave him his small case and he balanced it across his knees.

'You *are* well prepared,' he muttered. 'But I *can* walk, you know.'

'We know,' said Eddie. 'But it's a bit of a way and we've got to go fast—and then you've got to save your energy for the last bit.'

'Any chance you're going to tell me where we're going?' asked Uncle Wilf.

'That would spoil the surprise,' said Gwerren, taking his hand as Eddie began pushing the wheelchair.

Uncle Wilf looked up at her, his eyes adjusting to the faint luminobe glow, and he said something to her that made Eddie blink with surprise. He said, 'I know you, don't I?' Gwerren just smiled back at him. She didn't say anything.

No cars passed them as they made their way to the community hall. As they reached the car park adjacent to it Eddie took the backpack off and the street lamps suddenly came on.

'Good,' said Gwerren. 'Just in time.' The 'DANCE ALL OVER THE WORLD' poster was still up, gleaming.

'Come on,' said Eddie, digging into the backpack. 'The taxi will be here in five minutes. We need to be ready.'

Uncle Wilf sat back in his chair, staring in astonishment as Eddie and Gwerren transformed themselves. Out of the bag came two glittery wigs, assorted stick-on jewels, and sparkly make-up—even a hand mirror.

'Right, you go first.' Eddie handed the mirror and the glitter make-up to Gwerren and, sitting on the low wall of the car park, she began slapping it on over her eyelids and cheekbones and lips. Then she pulled the glitter wig on, tucking her long pale hair up into it. Eddie handed her a shimmering gold cape, too. And some sandals with sequinned straps, which she fumbled with. She had not been wearing any shoes at all. Eddie got his own wig on, and then grabbed the mirror and the make-up. Two minutes later he looked like a disco queen. Well—if you didn't look too hard. There was no sign of his ginger hair and his trainers were covered by a fringe of shiny red stuff which fell like a Christmas decoration from around each ankle.

'How about the voice?' he squeaked, trying to sound like Kayleigh. 'I'm gonna dance myself dizzy!'

221

Gwerren and Uncle Wilf smothered giggles as a lone car approached.

'We're all late leaving the dance contest,' Eddie explained hurriedly to Uncle Wilf. 'We've been helping to clear up. You did the Senior's Dance section and you're really tired. OK?'

'Whatever you say, Eddie!' chuckled Uncle Wilf. Whether or not he believed in Eddie's adventure, he was obviously having a great time.

'Taxi for Mr Smith plus two?' called the driver, his window winding down.

'That's us,' said Uncle Wilf, getting up. 'Me and my disco-dancing grand-daughters. Fancy me and two lovely young ladies being out so late, eh?'

The cab driver helped them put the folded wheel-chair in the large boot of the taxi and then they got into the back seat. Eddie dug the £20 note out of his pocket. He hoped it would be enough.

'Did you two win anything, then?' asked the driver, cheerily, peering back at them in his rear-view mirror.

'No,' said Gwerren. 'We're not that good.'

'Well you certainly look the part! Where to?'

'Wookey Hole village,' squeaked Eddie. 'You can drop us by the post office.'

'A bit of a late night for a kid's contest, isn't it?'

'Oh, we helped to get everything cleared up after-wards,' said Gwerren. 'It took ages!'

Happily the taxi driver didn't keep asking questions. Ten minutes later he dropped them at Wookey Hole village's small post office. As soon as he'd driven away, with just half of Eddie's money, they moved on down the road with Uncle Wilf back in the wheelchair. He was looking more and more astonished as they made their way along the River Axe and on towards the caves.

'Are we going where I think we're going?' he asked. 'In the dead of night? Are you two loopy?'

'Trust us,' said Eddie, although he was feeling very nervous now. He had been elated as the taxi had driven off—unable to believe the plan had worked this far. Any taxi driver who might be questioned about unusual middle-of-the-night fares would only be able to remember two very glittery girls of about eleven or twelve and an old bloke in a wheelchair who kept his hat well down over his face. Certainly not one old man and a ginger-haired boy.

But now, how were they going to get Uncle Wilf inside the caves and all the way down to Cartraethia? Eddie bit his lip. It took *him* long enough to reach the warm cave and he knew that Cartraethia was far, far lower than that.

Gwerren, though, seemed very relaxed. She helped Eddie push the wheelchair up the steep path towards the caves but then she stopped as they reached the covered walkway that led to the entrance and instead indicated a route up through the trees. Uncle Wilf looked uncertain. 'It's all right, Mr Harrison,' she said. 'You only need to walk a little bit further, up this slope. Then you can rest easy the whole way down.'

Uncle Wilf stood up and looked at her. 'I *do* know you, don't I?' he said. 'I know . . . your *light*.'

Gwerren smiled at him again. 'We haven't met—but I have seen your picture. And yes, you do know my light.'

'What are you two talking about?' hissed Eddie.

'Come on,' said Gwerren. 'They'll be waiting.'

Leaving the wheelchair on the path, they climbed the wooded slope more quickly than Eddie would have thought possible for Uncle Wilf. The old man was puffing and needed a steadying arm more than once, but a few minutes later they came out beyond the trees. Eddie gasped and felt the hairs on the back of his neck stand up.

Now he understood the rumours. Standing still on the crest of the hill, each in its own pool of unearthly blue light, were six ghosts.

224

Chapter 20

A gust of wind shook the low shrubs behind the ghosts and whipped their white hair across their faces. They were men ghosts, wearing what looked like animal skins fashioned into shorts and vests. Two of them carried something between them. Eddie stared at it, his heart clattering in his chest. It was a chair. A wooden chair.

'It's true,' Uncle Wilf was murmuring. 'It's really true! The ghostly Mendip hunters, still chasing deer and wild boar across the hills at night . . . I never thought I would see it with my own eyes. Eddie—was this what you brought me to see? One last adventure? Is this why you kept coming over here? You'd seen the ghosts of the Mendip hunters?'

'Nope,' gulped Eddie. 'I've never seen any ghosts! I come in the day, remember?'

'Oh really, you're both too silly,' said Gwerren

and then she waved at the ghosts. 'Come on!' she yelled. 'Give us a hand then!'

And instead of vanishing into thin air, the ghosts started running. Eddie and Uncle Wilf clutched at each other, gasping with fear. But as the spectres drew closer Eddie realized that they were not drifting through the air; their feet were connecting with the turf in a most un-ghostlike way. The closer they got the more solid they looked and at least two of them were grinning. They were completely silent though, and it was only as they got within a few feet of Eddie, Uncle Wilf, and Gwerren that they could be heard at all.

'Hello, Wren. You managed to get him here, then,' said one of the ghosts who had been grinning. Up close he was not a ghost at all, of course. Eddie could see he was as solid as Gwerren, with the same pale colouring and a luminobe tucked onto his shoulder. Gwerren grinned back at him and nodded.

'Here he is. And to think you didn't believe he was real!'

The man, who was full grown but not very tall, stepped across to Uncle Wilf and offered his hand. 'Wilfred Harrison. We are very pleased to meet you. Are you ready to come to Cartraethia? You are most eagerly anticipated.'

'You—you want me to go with you?' said Uncle

Wilf, shaking the proffered hand and staring at the man.

'If you wish it, certainly,' said the man. 'I am chief hunter Brennath. I know your world by night. I bring my hunters Twubuv once or twice a month. It is a beautiful place, but Cartraethia is more beautiful still. You have been named as welcome. Do you wish it?'

Uncle Wilf opened his mouth and just stared at Brennath. Then he looked at Gwerren and Eddie. 'Do I wish it?'

'You do,' said Eddie. 'It's wonderful!'

Uncle Wilf looked back at Brennath. 'I know your light,' he said. 'I know it.'

Something about the way he spoke made the hairs prickle across Eddie's skin.

'Come on then,' said Gwerren. 'If we stand up here much longer we'll scare the Overners and they'll send another priest!'

The men with the chair stepped forward and indicated that Uncle Wilf should sit, which he did, staring around at them in fascination. Eddie held on to his small case and Uncle Wilf settled back, his head resting on the high woven back of the chair, and then the men set off, lifting him up and tilting him gently back as they bore him smoothly along. They moved like wild

227

animals, fluidly and silently, as if the weight of the old man was no more than a few leaves in a bag.

Eddie and Gwerren ran along behind. 'What you said, then, about sending another priest,' puffed Eddie. 'Do you mean that Overners have sent them to exorcize you or something?'

'Oh yes,' chuckled Gwerren. 'All the time! Well, every few years in any case, whenever there's a sighting and they think we're ghosts. Brennath's very careful, though, and there's been no major sighting for a long time. But priests show up from time to time, trying to banish the spirits, the ghosts, the witches. It's quite sweet really—all that praying for our souls and splashing around of holy water. We don't mind, but it does put the poor priest to so much trouble.'

Eddie had a sudden flashback to the guide's talk in the first chamber of the caves. 'Wait a minute,' he said, trying to run as well as Gwerren and still talk, 'are you telling me the famous Witch of Wookey was one of you lot as well?'

'Oh, Meg! Yes—that was Meg,' said Gwerren. 'They used to call her High Chamber Meg because she was a bit of a loner and liked to be up in the high caves by herself a lot. I think she also liked scaring the locals. She was a bit naughty that way.'

'B-but—the priest came and chased her and turned

her into the rock,' spluttered Eddie. 'He threw holy water on her and all that.'

'Yes,' laughed Gwerren. 'She was most put out. But she didn't turn into stone, obviously. Really, Eddie—aren't you a bit old to be believing in that? She just ran back down to the Stratas and stopped trying to scare Overners. Good thing too. Very silly behaviour.'

Eddie was laughing now. Of course he had known that the Witch of Wookey story was a legend—even the guides smiled as they told it. It was still incredible, though, to think that the old hermit woman the locals feared was actually one of Gwerren's people. 'So—she didn't eat children, then?' he grinned. Gwerren just gave him a pitying look.

They came to a rock wall in the dip of a small valley and all at once, in a glimmer of luminobe, it was an open doorway. Uncle Wilf murmured aloud with surprise, but did not ask to get out of his chair as the hunters carried him into the passage. He simply glanced back at Eddie for reassurance and Eddie smiled and nodded, close behind him.

The journey to Cartraethia took nearly an hour. Eddie realized he and Gwerren would have done it in much less time but the hunters, swift and surefooted as they were, were deliberately taking time, to be sure that Uncle Wilf was comfortable and relaxed. They stopped several times in chambers of great beauty or interest, so the old man could stare around him and marvel at the stalactites or the whirlpools and waterfalls. Eddie felt proud, as if this was his own domain, and found himself just beaming wherever they stopped.

As they rested in a low-ceilinged chamber with a petrified limestone waterfall beneath a host of tiny straw formations which dripped delicately like the slowest rainfall, Uncle Wilf looked at Eddie and said, 'This isn't just a visit, is it, Eddie?'

'Not necessarily,' said Eddie.

'I think I may have died in the night,' said Uncle Wilf. 'We're going to the after life, aren't we? You shouldn't be here, though, should you? You've got a great long life ahead of you.'

'We *are* going to heaven,' said Eddie, 'but you're not dead.' And he leaned across and tugged hard on Uncle Wilf's ear. 'See—that still hurts, doesn't it? You don't feel that if you're dead!'

'Yes—thanks very much!' muttered Uncle Wilf, looking rather affronted—but at least it knocked the '*I'm only here in spirit*' look off his face.

When they finally reached Cartraethia again, Eddie felt a huge thrill. Since his last visit he had come to believe that maybe he had imagined some of its incredible size and beauty. He had been recovering from a near-death experience, after all, and probably his brain was a bit messed up. But no—the small town was as wonderful as he remembered, laid out in the valley of subterranean rock, its small hexagonal dwellings clustered along winding roads and the banks of the river, the warm pools still sending up aromatic steam here and there, a few people still going about their business contentedly, softly lit by the luminobes, glowing high in the stalactites above them and dotted all around the landscape below. Eddie noticed that the light was dimmer and less colourful than before and there was a quieter feel to the town. He guessed this was Cartraethian night, even though this land was not affected by night and day in the same way as his own world.

They had all paused at Angrid's little house, where he had been looked after by the old lady and by Gwerren. The hunters set down Uncle Wilf's chair and he stood up, his face awash with wonder, walked quite steadily to the wooden railing, leant his elbows on it, and stared and stared and stared.

The hunters walked on down the path, except Brennath, who stayed at Uncle Wilf's side, watching him with as much fascination as Uncle Wilf was displaying for Cartraethia. They stood, all four of them, for many minutes, as Uncle Wilf drank in the view and the smell and the sounds.

Finally Brennath said: 'Do you think it's time, then, Gwerren?'

Gwerren nodded. 'I'll go and get her. I'm sure she can hardly bear to wait much longer.'

And she walked to Angrid's dwelling and went through the door. Eddie stared after her, puzzled, and then saw, a minute later, Angrid walk from the house, with Gwerren emerging a few steps behind her. The look on Angrid's face was not what he had been expecting. He had thought the old lady would be smiling and welcoming, and she was, but she was also—*nervous*. Very nervous. She looked as if she did not know what to expect from the stranger who had been brought to her world. And yet she also looked as if she . . . as if she *knew* him.

Eddie touched Uncle Wilf's shoulder and he dragged his entranced gaze away from the vista of Cartraethia and turned to the woman who was approaching. And then his mouth fell open and his eyes widened and his breath hitched raggedly through his chest. He clasped the wooden rail with one hand and his throat with the other.

Angrid stepped closer and looked long and hard into his eyes. Her own were a little wet and she was also fighting some strong emotion, clasping her hands tightly together and gulping. 'Hello, Wilf,' she said, at length. 'It's been a long time.'

Uncle Wilf's face creased into a smile and tears flowed from his eyes unchecked. 'They didn't believe me,' he whispered. 'They told me you weren't real. They said I'd gone mad from the war and the prison camp. But I always knew—I *knew* you were real.'

'I'm so sorry I didn't return to you,' said Angrid. *Ann—of course. Ann! thought Eddie, in amazement. He could see her in the picture now—a young Angrid smiling in the dim light. Luminobe light.* 'When you didn't come for so long, I thought you had found an Overner girl. I waited for three years and then I believed I had lost you and I couldn't stand to know it for sure. So I stopped going Twubuv. And here I have stayed. And I thought you were long, long lost to me.'

Uncle Wilf pulled Angrid into his arms and held her tight. She wound her hands around his shoulders and neck, laid her head on his chest and closed her eyes. 'It's all fine now,' she sighed. 'You're back. You're with me. You're home.'

'Ooooooooh yeeeeeeessssss,' sighed Eddie. He was floating at the edge of one of the thermal pools and the water was as hot as a bath; hotter than the pool he had swum in with Gwerren in the warm cave last week.

'Ooooooooh yeeeeeeesssss,' echoed Uncle Wilf on the other side of the pool. Angrid slid in next to him. They were both wearing woven Strata-style bathing suits. Uncle Wilf's face was suffused with delight and healthy colour and he moved like a man ten years younger. And he had only been in Cartraethia for two hours.

'I really am going to have to go back,' said Eddie. 'In just a few minutes.'

'Yes, you are.' Gwerren sat on the bank of the pool and dipped her feet in. She smiled. 'But you can come back again. Now that you are welcomed, as much as Wilfred Harrison, you can come again, some-times. Although I will still want to play in the higher caves too. They are more adventurous.'

'How can anything be more adventurous than this?' asked Eddie, waving dripping fingers at the fabulous scenery around them. Above them some kind of lime-green fern sprouted from an overhang of rock, and little green ropes of some other kind of plant hung beneath it, dotted with tiny yellow flowers which smelt of honey.

'Well, this is home—the top caves are near Twubuv! That's really adventurous. Most of the people here will never go Twubuv. Only the hunters go and one like me, in every generation.'

'One like you?'

'Yes,' Gwerren kicked her feet out and a little fountain of water played in the air for a second or two. 'I am the Underner Sentinel. Or I will be. I work with Stan. He is our Overner Sentinel.'

'What on earth is that?' Eddie laughed. It all sounded very dramatic, while he was steaming away nicely in the pool. He had been delighted to find his swimming trunks still tucked into his backpack, so he could avoid the bathing suit offered to him by Angrid.

'We need people Twubuv,' explained Gwerren. 'Not many—just one or two at most. To keep us informed. They must be good and decent and brave and trustworthy beyond all doubt. Stan is like this. So he has been our Overner Sentinel for many years. But he must work with one of us—and I am that one. Or will be. I am training to be Cartraethia's sentinel. When Angrid properly retires I will live in her topmost dwelling and take over properly. Although I've been doing it for years anyway . . . '

'So was Angrid the sentinel when she met Uncle Wilf?' asked Eddie, turning over onto his front so he could rest his chin on his folded arms and look at Gwerren.

235

'Yes. She didn't bring him into the caves, but she saw a lot of him on walks through the gorges and hills. She met him up there one evening. He told her about the stars. He was out on a training exercise and using the night sky to navigate. She fell in love with him straight away. She thought he might be our next Overner Sentinel, until he left. Later she found Stan and he became the next Overner Sentinel instead. Stan married her sister—my gran. They lived together here for many years, but Stan always had to have a life Twubuv too. An Overner Sentinel must. When my gran died he went back Twubuv, to his bungalow in the village—but he stayed on for us as Overner Sentinel. He's ready to retire soon, though. Well, in the next few years. Maybe. He's been saying it for a long time but it never happens.'

Eddie got up out of the pool reluctantly and looked across at the reunited lovers. Angrid was kissing Uncle Wilf on the nose. 'She does look like you,' he said.

'My gran and she were twins,' explained Gwerren. 'They all say I look just like Angrid did at my age.'

'So that's why Wilf thought he knew you. And your light. He must have seen Angrid by luminobe light, all those years ago.'

'You really have to go,' smiled Gwerren.

Eddie said goodbye to Uncle Wilf and the old man, looking less old than ever, shook his hand. 'Will I see you again?' he asked.

'Yes! Of course!' said Eddie. 'But now I've got to get back to the house and watch all the fun.'

Uncle Wilf grinned. 'Tell them I've run off to be with my lover! That'll make your aunt choke on her toast!'

Chapter 21

When Eddie crept back into bed at just after 4 a.m. the dawn was already filtering through the curtains in Damon's room. He lay for a while, grinning up at the ceiling. He could not believe what he and Gwerren had done. They had *rescued* Uncle Wilf! They had done it! And reunited him with his long-lost love.

It was hard to imagine how anyone could be thankful for falling down a pothole to almost certain death, but Eddie was. If he hadn't tumbled through to the underground stream he would not have needed rescuing by Gwerren and she might never have felt she should take him to Cartraethia. On the long climb back up, she had told him that her luminobe had alerted her to his presence in the caves that day and she had at first thought he was at the usual place, in the Witch's Kitchen, which was why she had taken a longer time to reach him. Then she had needed to work out how

238

to get to him in his remote pothole. The journey through to his position in the underground stream was awkward, but she had persisted, sensing danger for him. She had had to hold her breath and go under water to get the rock off his foot. With water all around it by then, it had been easier to move. Then she had hauled him out of the water and sent a message for help from her luminobe to her great-aunt's. It seemed that luminobes were telepathic with each other—along with their other useful qualities. Brennath and two of his hunters had come and helped her carry the boy from Twubuv down to Cartraethia, where Angrid had looked after him.

Eddie pictured Uncle Wilf, lying happily in the steaming pool with Angrid, and smiled himself to sleep.

'EDDIE! EDDIE! WAKE UP!' His aunt was staring down at him crossly and for a moment he completely forgot why this might be.

'EDDIE!' she barked again. 'Do you know anything about Uncle Wilf?'

Blearily, he sat up and stared at her. 'Um . . . he's a war hero. He's eighty-eight. He likes *Countdown* . . . '

'Don't be stupid! I mean, do you know where

he's gone?' She looked much more annoyed than worried, he thought.

'He's gone somewhere?' he echoed. He wanted to laugh. He wanted to clap his hands together and hoot with laughter right into her face, but he couldn't, so he bit his lip and stared into his duvet.

'Yes! He's disappeared. And he's due at Cedar View in an hour! They will not like this. He could lose his place. He'd better come back in time,' she rumbled, ominously. 'Did he tell you where he was going? I mean, you're always in there with him, listening to him droning on about the war—I thought he might have told you.'

Eddie noticed how his aunt's thin veil of niceness was completely gone now. She was too annoyed to bother with it.

'He did say something about running away with his lover,' said Eddie, desperately suppressing his mirth.

'Oh, for heaven's sake! Now he's gone and lost his marbles,' she muttered. 'They might not take him if he starts ranting on about his ghostly girlfriend again. Honestly! After all the sacrifices I've made for him! This is how he repays me. Right! Get up! You have to help me search for him.'

Eddie scrambled out of bed, still bursting to laugh, but fortunately his aunt had left the room and was stomping back down the stairs, shouting at the twins to help too. Damon was still buried under his quilt, but he revealed a gummy eye and said, 'Wotchu laughing at?'

Eddie shook his head, his face pink with mirth. 'You'd never understand, Damon. You'd never understand.'

'Dipstick,' said Damon.

'Git,' said Eddie. He no longer cared about Damon hitting him. He would struggle with a sprained wrist, anyway, but Eddie wouldn't be able to stop laughing even if he got a smack in the face from his cousin's *left* hand.

Damon just disappeared back under his bedding and Eddie got washed fast, threw his clothes on, and hurried downstairs to enjoy his aunt's annoyance.

'He's taken his case!' she said to Eddie, as if it was *his* fault. Which, of course, it was—but she couldn't possibly know that. 'Go on—run along the road and see if you can find him. He can't have got far. If you can't find him I'll have to phone the police and report him missing. Oh, it's just too much!'

Eddie ran up and down the road, for effect, and even stopped at the corner shop to ask the nice lady if she had seen Uncle Wilf. 'Not for a year or more,' she said. 'He used to pop in for his paper once in a while, but no—not for ages.'

When he got back home, Auntie Kath was on the phone, looking pink and sweaty. 'Just a bit of a delay,' she was saying. 'No, he very much wants to come to Cedar View—he's been telling me how much he's looking forward to the bingo. We just need a couple more hours to get him ready. OK—see you at lunchtime!' She slammed the phone down and stared at Eddie. 'Well?'

'Nobody's seen him,' said Eddie. 'I think he's really gone for good.'

'Nonsense. He'll be on a park bench somewhere, missing his armchair and wishing he'd not been such an old fool,' snapped his aunt. 'Right. I'm phoning the police.'

The police came, eventually, at about tea time. It took them a while to take Auntie Kath seriously, especially as she came over all girly and breathy when she saw the men in uniform at her door. She made out that she was desperately worried about 'poor Uncle'. The police officers said they would put out an alert across the county, and they expected to find him quite soon. He couldn't have gone far. He certainly wouldn't have made it up the hills. Eddie grinned to himself as he remembered the Cartraethian hunters running across the Mendips with Uncle Wilf in his chair.

Auntie Kath phoned the rest home again, and rearranged delivery of their new resident for the following day. Eddie wondered how long she would spin it out before she had to tell them the truth.

'I don't know what you're looking so happy about,' said his aunt after tea that evening. 'I would have thought you'd be really worried.'

'I would be,' said Eddie. 'But I reckon he really has run off with his lover.'

'Well then, you're a bigger fool than he is! You won't be so chirpy when they find him dead in a ditch, stupid old man.'

Eddie's mum phoned that evening. 'Sweetheart, I want you to come home,' she said. 'I am so much better and I cannot wait to have you back. Dad and I think we should have the last couple of weeks with you before you go back to school. How about the Isle of Wight? We could go to Steephill Cove again.'

Eddie stood in the hallway, awash with emotion. Several different emotions. Just a few days ago he had lain under water, seeing his mum in his mind for what he thought was the last time. He desperately wanted to see her again; to hug her and feel that she was going to be OK at last. He wanted his dad's steady strength and good sense. He wanted to make up silly songs with them and watch nature programmes and yes—go to the Isle of Wight and poke about on the beach with them.

Now that Uncle Wilf had gone he couldn't wait to get away from Auntie Kath and his tiresome cousins—back to his own room and his own bed.

But, with a dreadful pang, he also realized that he really did *not* want to leave Gwerren and Angrid and the people of Cartraethia behind. He hadn't even begun to explore the secret underground world he had discovered—and he wanted to know how Uncle Wilf was getting along, of course.

'Eddie? Are you there?' his mum prodded, with laughter in her voice.

'Yes—I'm—I'm just . . . ' He felt his throat constrict. 'I really want to come home,' he said. And it was true. But it was also true that he wanted to stay. 'When will you come for me?'

'Tomorrow teatime, if that's OK. I've told your Auntie Kath.'

Eddie closed his eyes. Yes. It was OK. It was better than OK. But he wished he could stop time and just have a little more of it in Gwerren's world first.

'Yes. Please come,' he said. When he put down the phone and stared at himself in the hallway mirror, he seemed to see Gwerren staring back at him, and giving him a sad wave, luminobe glowing at her shoulder. At once, he made for the door. He had to see her again.

'Where do you think you're going?' asked Auntie Kath. 'I'm not losing any more family members this weekend, thank you! You stay put. Come and watch TV like a normal person.'

The next morning he tried to get out again, but now his aunt was making him pack and tidy up his end of Damon's room. She was also continually phoning up the police to ask if they'd found Uncle Wilf, and then asking Eddie again and again if he knew anything.

'He's with his lover,' said Eddie, several times.

'Well, you believe that if you want to,' she muttered.

By late afternoon there were bulletins on the local radio about Uncle Wilf, and she had to admit to the nursing home that he'd gone. She stood with the phone to her ear and her mouth tightly pursed as Barbara at Cedar View told her that they couldn't keep his place open for longer than two weeks.

Eddie eyed the door again, as soon as his bags were packed, late that morning. He had only hours before Mum and Dad arrived. He *must* get back to Gwerren before then. He could not just vanish from her life without explaining. But how could he get away now? As Kayleigh practised her disco song and dance routine up and down the hallway, wailing that she loved to love, but her baby just loved to dance, Eddie edged past her into the kitchen and asked Auntie Kath for one last wander on the hills with his bird books and binoculars. It was no good.

'Eddie, really! In the last two weeks I've nearly lost my son, had to deal with you being missing for hours, and now I've lost Uncle Wilf! You could show a bit of understanding,' she huffed. 'You're not going wandering off on your own and that's that. Oh, Kayleigh, will you *shut up*?'

Kayleigh stopped, mid squeak and shimmy, and burst into tears. 'You're horrible!' she shouted and ran upstairs, sobbing dramatically. Damon cackled from his seat in the lounge.

His rescue came most unexpectedly when the doorbell rang. Auntie Kath flew to it, hoping for news of her runaway uncle, and then stepped back in surprise. 'Oh, hello again!'

Peering round the kitchen door, Eddie was delighted to see Chris. 'I heard you were having a bit of a crisis with Uncle Wilf,' he said.

'Oh! Heavens, yes! Do come in,' said Auntie Kath, ushering the caver along the hallway and into the kitchen, where Eddie leaned against the fridge and grinned at him. 'Can you believe it? We were all set up for him to move to the *lovely* Cedar View and then this happens. I can't believe it. After all I've done for him!'

'How did you find out?' asked Eddie, as Auntie Kath flicked the switch on the kettle and put a teabag in a mug for her visitor. 'Did you hear about it on the radio?'

'No—I was duty solicitor for the cells at Wells police station yesterday,' said Chris. 'I was there when the report came through. I thought I remembered the name—and then, of course, I recognized the address. You must be terribly worried.'

'Oh we are. It's been more than twenty-four hours now—and you can't help but fear the worst,' sighed Auntie Kath, with drama. She added milk and handed him his tea.

'Of course, it must be difficult for you,' he smiled at her. 'I suppose the police have already asked for all his banking details, to check to see if he took out any money from his account?'

Auntie Kath looked suddenly edgy. 'Well . . . um . . . no, not yet. Do you think they will?'

'Well, yes—it's standard practice. A way of tracing him. If he is planning to go somewhere, he will want

247

to draw money out, won't he? I assume he has some savings.'

Auntie Kath looked edgier still. 'Well . . . not as such. I mean . . . of course there was some money but a lot of it was spent. And . . . '

Chris gave her a sympathetic look. 'As a friend, I should tell you that there probably will be a request to look through all his bank details,' he said. 'And— look—I may be talking out of turn, but just in case any savings were moved, into another account, perhaps to save them from being eaten up by care home fees— well—it might be a good idea to be straight about that.'

Auntie Kath sank down in the seat opposite Chris. She put her hand to her throat and looked flushed. 'It's not at all unusual for families to try to help,' went on Chris after a sip of tea. 'They do what they can to help their old folk hang on to their money—who wouldn't? Often they move it right across to their own bank accounts to keep it safe. So—if, by any chance, that's the case—better be straight. Don't want anyone thinking you bumped off poor old Wilf for his cash, do you?' He chuckled, but Auntie Kath looked across at him, stricken, and now paling.

'Well—that's exactly what we did do!' she whispered. 'Put his savings in another account, I mean. Just to look after it for him. And, well, I suppose that will be traced and I would hate anyone to think . . . I mean! Uncle Wilf *knew*, of course! He agreed to— no—he *asked* us to help him with it. But, of course, since then he's got a bit confused and I don't know if he'd remember that.'

'I would just pop it straight back across to his account right away,' advised Chris. 'You will get asked why, of course, but just tell them what you told me. Say you were a bit confused by how the care home thing works. That you thought it was free, because he's a war hero and it's council run and all that. Though of course, Uncle Wilf *would* have had to pay a bit in, if they'd known he had savings.

'Anyway—hopefully he'll turn up today and you won't have to worry about it at all. You can phone the bank right now—they're on the end of the phone seven days a week now, aren't they?'

'Yes—yes! I'll do it right away,' said Auntie Kath, grabbing the phone.

Eddie grinned at Chris. The man was amazing! 'I'm going home today,' he said.

'That's a shame,' said Chris. 'I was going to ask if you wanted to see a new dig that's starting up at Ebbor Gorge. We think we've found a new pothole link to the cave system.'

'Can we look at it now?'

'If your aunt says it's OK.'

'Can I just go out for a bit with Chris?' asked Eddie, as his aunt pulled her box files of bank details out of a cupboard, looking sick and shaky.

'Yes, yes—go! Be back by four o'clock, though,' she said.

Chris and Eddie let themselves out. In the road, under the occasional spot of rain, they walked fast away from the house, and both let out a long sigh.

'I meant all that I said in there, Eddie,' said Chris. 'I don't want your aunt to get into trouble. Even though she probably deserves to, if she really has ripped Wilf off to the tune of sixty or seventy thousand pounds, like you say. I'm very surprised the council didn't dig around in the family's bank details a bit harder—they usually do when it comes to testing whether people can afford to pay for care for their elderly. But council staff don't always do everything they should. So, what do you think has happened to Uncle Wilf? Seems to me like you know something.'

Eddie looked at Chris. He didn't want to lie to him. 'I do know something,' he said. 'He is OK. He's safe. He found his old girlfriend. He's living with her now, but I promised I wouldn't say where.'

Chris stopped and looked back at him. He shook

his head and grinned. 'Well, that's a story that gives us all hope!'

They walked on a little further and then he added, 'But look, Eddie, you need to make him understand that he has to make contact with someone. Me, if he likes. He needs to settle his affairs before vanishing, or the police will keep looking for him and your aunt might be tempted to look after his money for him all over again. And she'll probably end up getting it all anyway, if he's missing, presumed dead, for long enough. What's more, she really might get suspected of murdering him—and that wouldn't be fair, would it?'

Eddie looked up at the hill path on the other side of the road. 'You're right,' he said. 'But if I am going to see him again, I have to go now. My mum and dad are coming at four o'clock, to take me home.'

Chris handed him a small card with his name and business address and phone number on it. Then he shook Eddie's hand. 'I am very pleased to have met you, Eddie,' he said. 'And I really hope we'll meet again. Tell Wilf he can trust me.'

Eddie nodded and shook Chris's hand firmly back. And then he ran across to the road to the hill path and began the race back to the caves.

251

Chapter 22

He reached the caves in record time, even though it began to rain hard on his face and he slithered on the steep banks more than once. He went first to the cave tours entrance, but a long, long queue snaked up the path towards it. The foot-and-mouth disease crisis had been declared over and now tourists were coming from all over the country. It would take him an hour or more to get in on a tour, even with his special pass. He turned back up the path and went higher up the valley, to the wall of rock some distance above it, through which he had left the caves three times. He now knew that it *was* a door; that the luminobe behind it was projecting the illusion of solid rock, as well as a sturdy force field. And that luminobe would know he was here and send a message to Gwerren's luminobe. He had only to wait a little while.

He pressed his hands against the rock, which

was spattered with dark splodges from the rain. 'Tell Gwerren I'm here!' he said to it. 'I'm here and I have to see her! I won't be able to come back another day.'

There was no change in the rock, although he had half hoped that it might melt away for him, recognizing him as welcome in Cartraethia. He sat down on the wiry grass at the foot of it, and waited, while the clouds rolled lower and darker and the rain fell harder. Minute after minute ticked by and nothing happened. He began to feel slightly desperate, seeing that it was now nearly 1 p.m., and his aunt would expect him back for lunch by now. Not that he really cared. As long as he was back by 4 p.m., that's all that was important.

He was getting soaked. And cold. He longed for the warmth of the caves and the people he cared about. And then there was movement—a ripple of light behind him—and he looked up to see Gwerren standing in the shadows of the cave passage, shielding her eyes with one hand. She was wearing her white dress again, and he remembered it was Sunday and she had probably been to her church and sung in the choir that morning. Maybe their singing had risen up through the chambers and mystified a tour guide and his party once more.

'So will you burn up like a vampire if you step outside the caves?' he said. 'Even in the rain?'

'I might,' she laughed. 'Maybe one evening I'll

come out with you. I'd like to see your world a little bit more—as you've seen mine.'

'I did want to show you stuff—up in Twubuv,' said Eddie. 'It would have been great to show you around.'

'Would have been?' repeated Gwerren. She looked at him hard from under her palm. 'You're going. Aren't you?'

He got up, nodding. 'My mum and dad are taking me home today. Mum's better. We're all going on a holiday together.'

'I'm so glad she's better,' said Gwerren. 'I can see it in your face. Some of the lines have gone from it. That's good.'

Eddie had had no idea any lines had been evident in his face—but Gwerren saw things he couldn't.

'I—I'm going to miss coming here,' he said, stepping through the rock door. 'And—seeing you.'

'Where do you want to go?' she asked, in a voice that was not very convincingly chirpy. 'The warm cave? The sliding cave? Or all the way to Cartraethia to see Uncle Wilf?'

'I wish we could just play,' said Eddie, 'but I have to see Uncle Wilf one last time.'

* * *

At three o'clock that afternoon, the rock face in the valley rippled and Eddie stepped out into it, blinking. It was still raining. He turned to say one last goodbye to Gwerren and then gasped in shock. She had followed him. Right out of the cave. Now she stood with the rain falling onto her head and splashing down onto her bare shoulders.

Her skin looked almost transparent beneath the dull grey light of the rainy day. Her hand was shielding her eyes again; in its shadow they looked violet and huge. Her hair was white, not blonde. She looked alien—and beautiful—in a way that made Eddie bite his lip and squeeze his hands into fists and look at the ground. He did not want to cry in front of her.

'Will I see you again, Eddie Villier?' she asked.

Eddie shook his head. 'I don't know. I don't think I'll get invited back to my aunt's house in a hurry.'

'Do you live so very far away?' Her voice sounded small.

'It takes about three hours to drive here. And I haven't got a car, of course. I can't drive myself. Not for another five years at least.'

'Well . . . Five years is not so long. Will you come back then?'

'You'll have forgotten me by then!' He tried to laugh, but it didn't really work.

'We don't forget,' said Gwerren. She took his hand and he looked at her at last. She was smiling and there were tears in her eyes. Rain dripped off her fingers. 'I think you will come back,' she said. 'And in five years I will be Underner Sentinel and maybe—maybe Stan will be ready to retire. If there is someone who might take his place as Overner Sentinel.'

She looked hard at him and he realized what she meant. He grinned and nodded. He felt suddenly very sure. 'I am coming back,' he said. 'And sooner than five years! I will find a way! I will!'

She stepped forward and hugged him. She smelt of rock and water and warmth. And then, in her fluid, sudden way, she turned and was back in the cave tunnel and the wall was solid rock with a fading blue glow. And then it was just solid rock. And the adventure was over.

Chapter 23

Four days after his mysterious disappearance, an eighty-eight-year-old man walked into a firm of solicitors in Wells and instructed the staff there to update his will and look after his affairs. To his surprise he found that he had savings of £74,352 in his bank account. He asked for it to be bequeathed to one Eddie Villier on his eighteenth birthday. He agreed that any important post could be received, opened, and dealt with on his behalf by one of the solicitors—a man called Chris Whitcombe—as he was likely to be travelling and not easy to get hold of. The mobile phone number he gave might not be much good. It was tricky to get a signal where he was going.

A police investigation into his disappearance was promptly called off and his relatives were informed that he was well, but not likely to visit them.

Ellen Villier heard about some of this from her

sister-in-law, when she answered her mobile phone while paddling in the gentle surf at Steephill Cove, during the last week of the summer holidays. 'Hey, Eddie! You'll never guess what!' she called across to her son as he held a small wriggling crab in his cupped palms. 'Uncle Wilf showed up! He's OK! But he's gone off travelling, now. Would you believe it? Who would have thought he'd be able to do that, at his age? And with all the arthritis too! Apparently he looked really well, according to that solicitor caver bloke you know.'

Eddie grinned. Uncle Wilf had looked ten years younger after just one day in Cartraethia.

'That's brilliant!' he said. 'Mum . . . do you think we could go back to the Mendips next holiday? You, me, and Dad? Not to stay with Auntie Kath, but in a holiday cottage or something? I'd love you to see the caves and you could do all your walking on the hills and get even fitter.'

His mum smiled and nodded, rubbing her hand across her short baby curls of auburn hair. 'Why not? If you're going to be a cave rescuer you'd better go back and get some practice, I suppose. No taking your harness off next time, though, eh? We don't want you falling into the bowels of the earth again, do we?'

'Well . . . maybe not falling there,' smiled Eddie. 'But I'm definitely going to get there somehow.'

Ali Sparkes was a journalist and BBC broadcaster until she chucked in the safe job to go dangerously freelance and try her hand at writing comedy scripts. Her first venture was as a comedy columnist on *Woman's Hour* and later on *Home Truths*. Not long after, she discovered her real love was writing children's fiction.

Ali grew up adoring adventure stories about kids who mess about in the woods and still likes to mess about in the woods herself whenever possible. She lives with her husband and two sons in Southampton, England. Check out www.alisparkes.com for the latest news on Ali's forthcoming books.

DISCOVER MORE EXCITING
ADVENTURES FROM

Ali Sparkes

1956

Freddy and Polly are used to helping their father with
his experiments. So they don't mind being put into
cryonic suspension—having their hearts frozen until
their father wakes them up again. They know it will
only be for an hour or two, so there's nothing to worry
about . . .

PRESENT DAY

Ben and Rachel have resigned themselves to a long,
boring summer. Then they find a hidden underground
vault in the garden containing two **frozen figures**, a
boy and a girl. And when Rachel accidentally presses a
button, something unbelievable happens . . .

*Can Polly and Freddy adapt to the twenty-first century?
Will their bodies survive having been in suspension for so
long? And most important of all, what happened to their
father—and why did he leave them* **frozen in time***?*

WHAT IF YOU HELD THE POWER OF THE UNIVERSE IN THE PALM OF YOUR HAND?

Ty Lewis is messing about in the woods when he stumbles upon something freaky—a glowing lump of rock or metal or *something*. Whatever it is, it gives him an amazing power.

Which is cool at first, until Ty's new powers start attracting attention, and soon he's being followed by two sinister agents who seem intent on 'collecting' him.

But Ty has no intention of letting that happen. So now he's got to RUN . . .

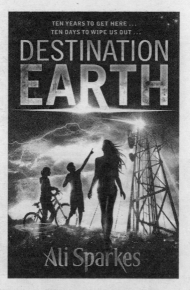

TEN YEARS TO GET HERE . . .
TEN DAYS TO WIPE US OUT . . .

Imagine you are the only **survivor** from another planet. You've spent ten years on a spaceship learning how to be human, and now the end of your journey is in sight . . .

All you have to do is land safely, convince the earthlings that you're a **real teenager**, and start your new life on Earth. No problem.

Except that the **killer alien** responsible for wiping out your people has hitched a lift. And it's just a matter of time before it starts on the human race . . .

UNLEASHED

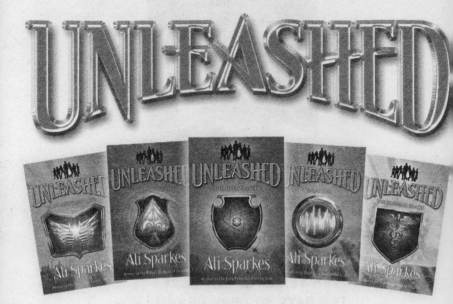

A group of very special teenagers. Each with an incredible power, they live together, protected by the government. Out in the ordinary world they know they must not use their powers. But good intentions are easy . . . following them through is another matter.

The fantastic *Unleashed* series is action-packed, with a pace that's non-stop. Read the entire series now . . .